HOT MESS

Into The Fire Series

J.H. CROIX

This is a work of fiction. Names, characters, businesses, places, events and incidents are either the products of the author's imagination or used in a fictitious manner. Any resemblance to actual persons, living or dead, or actual events is purely coincidental.

Copyright © 2018 J.H. Croix

All rights reserved.

ISBN-13: 978-1984057938

ISBN-10: 1984057936

Cover design by Cormar Covers

No part of this book may be reproduced in any form or by any electronic or mechanical means, including information storage and retrieval systems, without written permission from the author, except for the use of brief quotations in a book review.

❦ Created with Vellum

To the unexpected gifts life throws our way, occasionally known as accidents.

Sign up for my newsletter for information on new releases & get a FREE copy of one of my books!

http://jhcroixauthor.com/subscribe/

Follow me!
jhcroix@jhcroix.com
https://amazon.com/author/jhcroix
https://www.bookbub.com/authors/j-h-croix
https://www.facebook.com/jhcroix

HOT MESS

Ward

Susannah is the only woman who's ever tested my control. Fighting fires is my life, but I can't put out the fire between us.

I tell myself I can keep my distance, tell myself it's nothing more than a little fun. She fills every corner of my thoughts, kicks my control to the curb.

Still, I have this. I can handle her. Then I find out she's pregnant—with our baby.

All bets are off. I'll do anything to make her mine.

Susannah

One night. Four years ago. We nearly set each other on fire, but I never thought I'd see Ward again.

Then he comes walking back into my world—the epitome of tall, dark & dangerous. I can't take the heat. We take another chance, thinking we can burn this fire to ashes.

But that's only the beginning. It's a mess—he's my boss and now... He's about to be a father.

Chapter One
WARD

I stared across the room, unable to keep my eyes off of Susannah Gilmore. She was leaning against the polished wooden bar, her strawberry blonde hair spilling out in a mass of curls around her shoulders. I didn't know what the hell the bartender was saying to her, but I was instantly annoyed. The look in his eyes was one of blatant appreciation.

Not that I blamed him. Susannah was fucking gorgeous. Strong as hell, feisty as hell, and so damn sexy, it was a miracle I'd managed to keep my hands to myself the last few days.

I was in Willow Brook, Alaska to meet the hotshot firefighter crew I was about to join as superintendent. I was only here for one more night before returning to visit my mother. I'd almost rescheduled this trip because the original plan had been for me to start this week. That was before my mother was moved into hospice care earlier this week.

In the meantime, I intended to do one thing before I left for the month tomorrow morning—have another night with Susannah, a repeat of our last night when we both finished our hotshot training in California four years ago. That night was seared into my memory. I hadn't known what to expect when I learned she worked on the crew I'd be leading.

Four years was long enough for both of us to forget each other. Yet, I'd stepped into the station here and known she was in the room before I even saw her. My body was a tuning fork tuned solely to her. I'd been here for three days since, and the lust simmered on high the entire time. We couldn't be around each other without practically catching on fire.

I knew pursuing her wasn't smart. Hell, I was about to become her boss. Yet, I didn't particularly want to think smart right now. I wanted to forget everything else, and Susannah could help me do that.

I watched as the bartender turned away from Susannah to serve another customer. The crew had brought me with them to Wildlands Bar & Lodge, apparently a popular place, judging by how crowded it was. It was late, and most of the crew had left for the night. When it was clear the bartender was keeping busy, I took that moment to make my approach.

Leaning against the bar beside Susannah, I glanced to her. Simply being close to her, my body tightened further and my cock twitched. She didn't have to do a damn thing to turn me on. All she had to do was exist.

Her blue eyes caught mine as she looked over, a pink flush staining her cheeks.

"Ward, I thought you'd left for the night," she said.

I leaned on the bar with both elbows, if only to mask my aching arousal. Shaking my head, I held her rich blue gaze. "Not yet."

We stared at each other, the air humming around us, snapping and crackling with electricity. A few years back I'd been called up to help with a fire in the backcountry here in Alaska. I'd heard stories about the eruption of Mount Augustine back in the nineteen-eighties. According to a fellow firefighter I met, the ash had been thick and occasionally formed small clouds in the air where the particles from the volcano rubbed against each other, creating a mini electrical storm within the clouds.

I'd never seen anything like that myself, but the memory of it stuck with me. That was what it felt like when I was near Susannah.

She didn't say a word, but she didn't look away either. Her tongue darted out, swiping across her bottom lip.

After a moment, she spoke. "We're gonna have to figure this out."

"Figure what out?" I asked.

Her breath drew in sharply. I took the moment to just soak her in. She had freckles scattered across her porcelain cheeks, and her nose tipped up at the end. She was so damn gorgeous and endearing at once with this tomboy vibe I loved. I couldn't say why she hit me so hard. Hell, it wasn't as if I hadn't met other beautiful women. There weren't many female firefighters, yet she wasn't a complete anomaly. For me, she was. One look at her, and it was like a swift kick straight to my gut and my heart. She was a living, breathing shot of adrenaline and lust in my veins.

I understood her question. The bald truth was I was about to become the superintendent for her crew. As one of the crew foremen, she would answer directly to me once I was in my official capacity. Although I knew the reasoning behind her question, I wanted to make her say it. Because I wasn't in my official position yet and wouldn't be until I returned. I wasn't above admitting that the knowledge I'd be her boss only made me want her more. The fact our attraction shouldn't be happening only fed into its fire.

Susannah lifted her chin, not backing down or looking away. "You're taking over as superintendent for my crew. We need to forget about that night."

I held her gaze and shook my head slowly. "You can't make me forget anything, and I know you haven't forgotten either. In fact, I think maybe we should have another night like that. Tonight."

Her lips parted and her breath hissed through her teeth. I suppose she expected me to be proper. Fuck that. I knew who and what I wanted. Her. Bare naked and tangled up with me.

Her eyes darkened as she stared at me. For a moment, I thought she was going to tell me to fuck off, but she didn't. She nodded, just barely.

Snagging her drink off the bar, she downed it quickly. "Follow me."

"Lead the way," I replied.

She spun away, her cowboy boots striking on the hardwood floor as she strode quickly in front of me, her hips swinging with every step.

Chapter Two
SUSANNAH

I could feel the heat of Ward's gaze on me as I walked ahead of him. Threading my way through the tables, I barely registered the hum of voices around us. The bar was crowded, yet we might as well have been alone in a room. I turned into the hallway at the back, not waiting to see if he was behind me. My body knew he was with certainty. The air around us snapped with the force of the attraction between us. Any hopes I had that this yearning, burning fire between us would have dissipated had been dashed the moment he walked into the station the other day.

Ward Taylor had somehow managed to become even more attractive than the last time I'd seen him. I didn't know if that was a factual observation, but that was sure as hell how my body felt. Black curls, always slightly tousled, and those silver gray eyes, like the sky on a stormy summer day. One look from him, and it seared through me. His body was honed to perfection. I'd thought myself immune to men like him. As a hotshot firefighter, I spent my days with men in their physical prime. Yet, not a single man affected me the way Ward did.

Ward carried himself with an edge of danger, quiet strength, and simmering power under the surface. Back when I trained with him, he kept his distance from all of us. Oh, he was a good teammate, but there was a part of him he kept under wraps. I sensed something or someone had hurt him, yet I'd never scratched beneath the surface to understand more.

Despite trying damn hard to erase it from my memory, I'd never forgotten the night we'd had together. It was so far and above any other sexual experience I'd ever had, I couldn't imagine anything coming close. Three days with him around the station, passing by each other like flint to stone again and again—each pass striking another spark into the fire that just wouldn't die.

I'd been obsessing about how to handle the fact he was about to become my boss, while I was nearly melting at his feet every time we were anywhere near each other. A respite was on the horizon because Ward was leaving for a month since his mother was sick. Cade and Levi were going to help out until Ward could return. That was what they'd been doing all along since Al's retirement.

As it was, we had one cranky as hell crewmember who was flat pissed he hadn't gotten the job of superintendent. The rest of us on the crew had been relieved. Chad was an asshole. As far as I was concerned, Al should've fired him, but he hadn't. Ward was going to inherit that problem, although I felt like he was better suited to deal with it than our last superintendent.

Ward took no bullshit. It was all business at all times out in the field, and that was what we needed. Sad as I was to learn his mother was in hospice, even though Ward barely showed any emotion over it, it gave me some breathing room to figure out what the hell to do.

Yet right now, tonight, I was doing the craziest thing I could imagine. The moment Ward walked over and looked at me, I was a goner. I wanted him so fiercely. I was flat crazy for giving into it, but my need for him was rushing through me with such force, I couldn't ignore it. I was busy telling myself we could do this and then move on.

I knew little of Ward's personal life. He had a few friends when we were in training together. He was quiet and bordered on brooding. Unlike some of the other guys who liked to party and have a good time, he laid low. He certainly didn't do romance. In fact, our epic one-night stand had started with him pointing out it was perfect because we would never see each other again.

I couldn't even contemplate what he thought tonight might mean. As I walked down the hallway, which felt like forever, I could already feel the slick moisture soaking my panties. Just thinking about the memory of him sinking into me, every hard, thick inch of him, was enough to make me wild.

Ward knew how to use his hands, his lips, and his tongue so well, he'd left me boneless. He'd acquainted himself with every inch of my body, including my now dripping wet pussy, before fucking me until I forgot where I ended and he began.

Maybe one more round with him would burn my need to ashes.

As I passed by the restroom, I paused, turning to see him behind me. He ambled, his long stride eating up the distance between us with little effort.

"I'm going to use the restroom really quick, okay?"

His eyes burned through the distance between us as he nodded. He stopped in the hallway as I stepped inside, leaning against the door to catch my breath.

I didn't need to go to the bathroom, but I needed a moment to get a grip. I stared at myself in the mirror. My hair was a bit wild tonight, and my cheeks were flushed. I had a full body flush just from Ward's presence. Taking a deep breath, I splashed cool water on my face and washed my hands, my body nearly humming in anticipation with every passing moment.

When I stepped out, Ward was leaning against the wall across from the door, one hand hooked in his pocket and the other hanging loose at his side. He wore faded black jeans, battered leather black boots, and a navy T-shirt that outlined his sculpted chest and broad shoulders. My mouth went dry and my pulse took off, skittering wildly.

My breath came in shallow pants and my sex clenched as I stared at him. Perhaps two feet separated us. From across the hallway, he reached out and hooked his finger in my belt loop, pulling me flush against his body inside of a quick breath.

I liked to think of myself as a woman in control of her life, of her destiny, of her body and her mind. Most of the time, I was.

Except when it came to Ward. All of my defenses burned to nothing in the searing heat of his presence.

When my body bumped against his, I almost moaned aloud. I hadn't forgotten how good he felt—all hard strength, coiled energy and power. Even his face was strong with a square jaw, sculpted cheekbones, the dark slash of his brows over those silver gray eyes, and a nose that looked as if it had been broken once, giving him a roguish charm.

Ward wasn't much for smiling, which made it dangerous when he did. Like now. His lips curled at one corner with his eyes locked to mine.

My breath caught and my belly clenched.

He didn't say a word. One hand slid around to cup my bottom and pull me tight against him, the hard ridge of his arousal pressing into my belly and sending a gush of moisture into my panties. I didn't know if it was actually possible to orgasm simply from standing beside someone, but if anyone could make that happen, Ward could.

He lifted his other hand, brushing a loose curl off my

cheek and tucking it behind my ear. Goose bumps ran in a shiver down my side.

I could barely breathe, my body pulsing with anticipation. In a flash, he claimed my mouth with his. He kissed as boldly as I remembered, his hand palming my ass as he rocked his arousal into me, hard and insistent at the apex of my thighs.

Kissing him was like getting caught inside of a flame. His hand tangled roughly in my hair as he devoured my mouth. Deep sweeps of his tongue, drawing back to nip at my bottom lip. Inside of a matter of seconds, I was so caught up in our kiss, I completely forgot where we were, nudged out of my madness only when I heard the door to the hallway open from the parking lot.

My panties were drenched and my breath came in rough gasps. I broke free and stumbled away from him. My gaze swung wildly to the back doorway to see a cluster of people I didn't recognize entering. Thank God. The chances it could be someone I knew were high. I'd been born and raised in Willow Brook and knew most everyone local. But it was early spring, and the tourists were already crowding into town.

The group filed down the hallway between Ward and I. His eyes never left mine, my gaze drawn back to his like a magnet. The force of his gaze was so powerful, it felt as if he were actually touching me. After the customers made their way past us, their footsteps echoing on the hardwood floor and the sounds from the bar filtering into the hallway, he reached across the space between us again, catching my hand and reeling me close.

My brain tried to fire off a thought. But it was as if all of the signals were crossed, haywire in the heat of the desire between us. Flush against him again, my nipples tight, need pounding inside of me, and my breath barely under control, I couldn't manage a word.

"Let's go," he said, his gruff voice sending a prickle down my spine.

I nodded wordlessly. He turned, my hand held tight in his. I suddenly remembered what it felt like to be held by him—beyond the pounding need, there was more. This man, so handsome, so sexy he was dangerous, somehow made me feel safe. Though there was a distance to him, a wall I didn't know how to scale, I felt safer with him than I'd ever felt with anyone in my life.

Chapter Three
SUSANNAH

One month later

The little blue line stared at me, distinct and clear. There were three of them sitting in front of me on the bathroom counter. Three blue lines, all telling me the same thing. I had a fourth pregnancy test with me. Maybe I was crazy, but I wanted to be sure. Plus, I liked the number four. It was nice and even. I pulled the last test out of the box. With my heart pounding and anxiety spinning through me, I was almost sweating. I squatted over the toilet again—another undignified moment where I tried to direct my pee onto the little plastic stick.

Tugging my underwear and leggings up again, I looked at the test immediately, watching as the distinct blue line appeared. I still couldn't quite absorb the fact that I now had four drug store pregnancy tests telling me I was pregnant. My mind tumbled wildly, thoughts racing every which way, as I scrambled to make sense of this.

I can't be pregnant. This has to be a mistake.
Just go to the doctor, and you'll find out it's some weird fluke.

My mind lobbed these points back and forth, but my gut

instinct was reacting otherwise. I was never late for my period, but I was over a week late now. How the hell could I have gotten pregnant? I thought back to that night with Ward, just over a month ago. We had used a condom every time.

I flushed hot all over, just thinking about it now. Because that night had merely served to trump my other night with Ward. Over the four years that passed since the first night with him, I tried to convince myself my memories were exaggerated, that sex with him hadn't been that amazing.

My memories hadn't done the first night justice. Sex with Ward was a sensual feast. The entire night was a blur of sensation. We couldn't get enough of each other. Oh. My. God. He was insanely good in bed, a shattering mix of rough, demanding and gentle. If you had asked me before if I would've liked a man to take control the way he did, I would've laughed the idea off. Ward melted me, inside and out.

I forced my mind off this train of thought. I didn't need to recall how hot I was for Ward. Most definitely not. Not when I was facing a rather shocking reality. I was absolutely positive we'd used a condom every time, but I had four pregnancy tests with damning blue lines on the bathroom counter. I sat down on the toilet, tunneling my hands through my hair with a sigh.

I would go to the doctor to be absolutely certain. Yet, the evidence was fairly clear. I was almost one hundred percent certain I was pregnant, and Ward was the father.

Restless, I stood quickly, striding out of my bathroom to a small desk in the corner of the living room. Opening my laptop, I inanely searched *can you get pregnant with a condom?*

Great, just great. According to my trusty Internet search, even if we'd used every condom perfectly every time, there was still a two-percent chance of pregnancy. The overall statistic was even more sobering. In real life, condoms were effective a lowly eighty-five percent of the time. Because real life translated to how well people paid attention to detail when they were so hot for each other, they were practically on fire.

With a slow sigh, I closed my laptop and leaned back in my chair. I idly glanced around. I loved my small home. My father had helped me build it a few years back. My family owned lots of land in and around Willow Brook. My place was on a lovely few acres not too far from my parents' home. My father and I had built a cute A-frame cabin for me with decks on both floors. The downstairs living room area was bright and airy with windows comprising the entire front wall and overlooking a field with a view of Swan Lake in the distance.

The kitchen was toward the back of the downstairs with a bathroom and laundry off to one side. Upstairs, there was a loft with two bedrooms and a bathroom. The space was bright and open with modern, clean lines. I wanted a dog, but I kept holding off because I felt like my lifestyle didn't fit a dog very well. As a hotshot firefighter, I was gone for weeks at a time during the summer months.

All of a sudden, my mind skipped from a dog to a baby. The first thought that passed through my mind was relief I had two bedrooms because there would be a room for the baby. My thoughts came to a screeching halt, so screeching it was a miracle I didn't get whiplash from the force of it.

What the hell was I thinking? Was I seriously thinking about actually having a baby?

Apparently, I was. The gravity of my situation slammed into me, and I lost my breath for a moment. I would go to the doctor to be absolutely certain, but four pregnancy tests were shouting the answer loud and clear—I was pregnant.

I knew without a doubt that Ward didn't expect this. We had used protection every time. That night was just supposed to be one night, and then we'd forget about it. The following morning he had made me coffee, and the mood had been relaxed and easy. Somehow, I'd convinced myself we'd carry on without a hiccup. We'd even been all adult about it.

I'd said, "So when you get back, we forget this ever happened right?"

His silver gray eyes flashed. "Of course."

Now I was pregnant, and he was due back tomorrow. This was a colossal mess.

Chapter Four
WARD

"Here ya go," Rex Masters said as he handed me a cup of coffee.

I took a quick sip, savoring the flavor. "Thank you," I said with a nod.

Rex rounded his desk, gesturing towards the chair across from it as he sat down. I slipped into the chair, leaning back and shifting my shoulders to ease the tension that had been bundled there for the past month straight.

I'd buried my mother a week ago, and my younger brother had belatedly shown up for the funeral. I tried to remember the last time he had seen our mother before she died. I couldn't because I had figured it was best not to dwell on the past.

After the pain of watching cancer steal my mother, I had to deal with Dwight's resentment. To give him some credit, I think he felt badly he hadn't bothered to come see our mother in hospice. I'd been close to my mother, but otherwise, my family wasn't particularly close. One thing that bound us together was money and lots of it.

For that reason alone, I shouldn't have been surprised at

Dwight's appearance. Dwight's father had married my mother for her money and had been furious when he got none of it in the divorce. That detail had been a festering resentment for Dwight for years. Part of me would've been relieved if she'd left all of it to Dwight, if only to excise his resentment for once and for all. Yet, much as I didn't need the responsibility of dealing with it, I didn't care to watch Dwight blow through whatever he inherited.

She'd played it smart in her will. My mother wasn't a vengeful person, which was why I'd been so pissed at how Dwight essentially ignored her for years. She left him one of the family homes and a massive chunk of land in Bozeman, Montana, along with a small fund to be overseen by an executor. The fact his actual cash assets were overseen by someone else pissed him off. I'd had to listen to him bitch about it for days.

Thank God she had the sense to keep my inheritance private. Dwight could only guess at what he thought I might have inherited, although he'd made plenty of cutting comments about how I wouldn't have to work another day in my life. As if I had any desire to be that lazy.

I loved my job, and right now, I needed it. Being outdoors working would keep me focused on something other than the wheels spinning in my mind.

This past month had been rough. There was one memory I'd visited time and again when I wanted to banish everything I was facing—my last night with Susannah. I knew it was rational for me to keep a wall between us. But, dammit, I didn't want to.

I forced my attention back to Rex, taking another sip of coffee. Rex Masters was the Police Chief for Willow Brook. Willow Brook Fire & Rescue shared the station with his small force, and Rex essentially ran the station. Stepping in as a superintendent for one of the three crews based out of here, it would behoove me to get to know him.

Rex was easy going with a ready grin, which he cast my

way just now. "Good to see you. I'm sorry to hear about your mother," he said, his gaze sobering.

I took a sip of coffee to buy myself a moment and managed a nod. "Thank you. She meant a lot to me. It wasn't a surprise, although the timing was certainly bad."

Rex nodded politely. I trusted Rex on sight based on nothing more than a feeling he gave me. While I wasn't one to share much personally, I'd learned over the years if you kept too much to yourself, people had more questions. I'd learned to walk that line well, offering just enough.

"She was diagnosed with breast cancer two years ago. She fought it, but it was hard on her. We knew it was simply a matter of time. She was comfortable at the end, and that's all that mattered to me."

Rex was quiet, his gaze warm, before nodding slowly. "Well, that's about the best you can hope for. Do you have any other family?"

"A brother," was all I offered.

Rex didn't push for more. Like Dwight's father, my father had married my mother for her family's money. Unlike Dwight's father, my father got a tidy settlement in the divorce, and we never heard from him again. I had very few memories of him and that was perfectly fine with me.

I offered none of this to Rex, simply nodding again, thanking him for asking and deftly moving on. "So I understand you're the nerve center here at the station," I commented.

Rex chuckled, his eyes crinkling at the corners. "You could say that, although I would argue that's Maisie. You met her when you were here before, right?"

"Of course. She's the main dispatcher, right?"

"That she is. Her grandmother was our dispatcher for years. We have a few backups, but Maisie's the only full-time dispatcher. The Anchorage station covers the line during night shifts and then we have a weekend person. If you didn't catch it when you were here earlier, Maisie's married to Beck Steele, one of the other firefighters here," he explained.

"Oh right. Seems like a tight group here." I was also aware one of the other superintendents, Cade Masters, was Rex's son.

Rex leaned back in his chair, his gaze considering. "So it is. You signed on for a two year contract."

His words were a statement, yet I could sense the question contained within them.

"That I did. I enjoy the work. I was up here one summer with a crew from Montana, and I loved the area. When I saw the position open up, I decided to jump on it."

Rex eyed me thoughtfully. "Good. We requested the two years because this is a tightknit community, and relatively speaking, it's isolated. We needed a leader committed to being here for a bit."

"Absolutely understood. I didn't question it."

"I understand from Susannah Gilmore that you trained in California with her," he commented.

Simply the mention of Susannah's name sent a prickle of awareness through my body. If I were being honest with myself, I couldn't wait to see her again. In fact, I'd already come up with a rationale for why we should keep having nights like the one we had before I left last month.

But I couldn't exactly mention that to Rex. Instead, I nodded politely and took a sip of coffee.

"Susannah is an excellent crew member. You'll be glad to have her on your team," Rex said, setting his coffee down. He picked up a pen, twirling it idly in his fingers. "So I suppose I should fill you in on a few dynamics for the crew. One of the advantages I have being over here in the police part of the station is I have some separation from you guys. I usually know what's up though. Anyway, Chad Meyer has been a problem lately. Frankly, since he was hired. He's not what I'd call a team player. Honestly, he's an ass. He was a bit of a problem with Susannah at one point, on her about going out with him, but she kept her distance. When Al retired, Chad put in for the position. He's too clueless about how the rest of the crew perceives him to realize he didn't have a snowball's chance in hell. I advised against even bothering with an interview," Rex explained.

"So I'm guessing he's not too thrilled I'm here," I offered.

"Oh, it's not you. It's the position. It doesn't matter who got the job, he was going to be an ass about it. To be blunt, I thought Al should've fired him sooner, but I think he decided to put this one off because he was on his way out. Al's a great guy. He got injured about a year ago and lost the spark for the work. I wanted to give you that heads up about Chad because my guess is you're going to want to do something about him sooner rather than later. Aside from him, you're walking into a solid crew."

"Thanks for filling me in." I finished my coffee and stood, catching Rex's eyes. "I appreciate you being direct with me. I'll try to deal with it quickly. To be honest, I have zero patience with bullshit. Either you're committed to the team and your role on it, or you're not."

Rex nodded. "Sounds good to me. I've got your back on this if he tries to pull any bullshit in the meantime."

I nodded, although my thoughts were already drifting to Susannah. Hearing this guy had been on her case sent a wash of protectiveness rolling through me. It infuriated me to think the jerk tried to hit on Susannah. This train of thought should've been a wake up call for me, but it wasn't. It barely registered for me that I could lump myself in the same category. Yet, Susannah kicked rational thought to the curb in my brain.

Only one word came to mind when I thought of her.

Mine.

Chapter Five
SUSANNAH

I watched as Ward walked across the parking lot outside the station, his black curls tousled and his silver eyes piercing me from a good twenty feet away—ridiculously sexy and downright dangerous for my sanity.

He'd been back in Willow Brook for a full two days now, and by sheer luck, I'd managed to avoid being alone with him the entire time. He'd set up meetings with everyone on the crew, including me. I'd begged off with the excuse of a doctor's appointment—an entirely factual excuse. I did have a doctor's appointment. Yet, he'd lose his mind if he knew why.

Dr. Jensen confirmed what my four pregnancy tests had already told me—I was pregnant. She estimated me to be approximately four weeks along. It was easy to figure out when I'd gotten pregnant, seeing as I'd only had sex once in the entire past year, although I hadn't shared that rather depressing detail with her.

She'd been my OB/GYN for years now, so she knew me fairly well. When she'd asked me if I was excited, I'd promptly burst into tears. At which point, she realized that this pregnancy was a massive surprise.

She'd graciously asked me what I wanted to do and carefully explained my options. There would've been a time in my life when I would've been appreciative to consider options. Even though I was confused and conflicted about my circumstance, I knew with certainty I wanted to have this baby. And that? Well, that put me in a hot mess.

I didn't like to lie. I was a straightforward person, preferring to cut to the chase and cut through any bullshit. Yet, I had no idea how to talk to Ward about this. None. At all.

Not to mention, I didn't know how to deal with the small problem related to the spark that just wouldn't fucking quit between us. Every time I passed through his orbit in the station, my body felt electrified. Little bolts of lightning sent sparks scattering through me. And his eyes, those silver eyes flashing at me, the heat contained within them seared me inside and out.

From the look in his gaze, I was starting to get the sense he had no intention of forgetting what happened between us. Little did he know, there would be a huge reason that would make it impossible to forget.

Ward reached me, stopping a few feet away, the force of his presence setting a subtle vibration off inside of me. He was a strong man with a potent presence—all coiled strength and languid power. He didn't throw his weight around like some men did, as if they needed to prove their power. He was so damn confident, masculinity and power simply oozed from him.

The moment my gaze collided with his, I had to catch my breath as my pulse took off at a gallop. He stared at me, his eyes locked to mine and his gaze far too knowing for my comfort.

"Hi," I managed, that single word coming out breathy.

He was quiet for a beat, arching a brow. "You haven't met with me yet," he said, pointing out the obvious.

I nodded. "I know. Sorry about that. I really did have a doctor's appointment."

I was exceedingly relieved I wasn't lying about that detail. Truth aside, I was so uncomfortable because of why I had a doctor's appointment, I didn't know what else to say.

We were interrupted by the back door to the station opening. Cade and Beck walked out together. They parted ways, each going to their respective vehicles. Cade glanced over, giving a wave just as Beck called over a goodbye. I watched as they climbed into their trucks and drove away.

Ward and I were alone again, a fact of which my body was hyperaware. Butterflies spun in my belly, and liquid need slid through my veins. The effect he had on me was embarrassing.

"Have dinner with me," he said, his gruff voice sending a shiver over my skin.

Like an idiot, my head was bobbing along in a nod before I even thought about what my answer should've been. Definitely no. In fact, what I should've done was request to be assigned to a different crew post haste.

Of course, that didn't resolve the gigantic issue looming before me. I had to somehow find a way to tell Ward I was pregnant and planning to have our baby, a baby I was fairly certain he didn't want.

Before I could gather myself and backtrack, his mouth curled into a grin. Fuck me. He was dark and dangerous with a broody, rough edge to him. Throw in even a hint of humor, and I had no willpower to resist him. I didn't even want to. My belly promptly executed a flip as if on command, and my sex clenched.

Ward's presence could pull the strings on my body like nobody's business.

"Where?" he asked.

I was still scrambling to rectify my nod, but then I figured I'd look even more ridiculous if I tried to say no now. I almost said Wildlands, but if we were going to see anyone from our crew, it would be there at this time of day.

"Firehouse Café. Have you ever been there?"

"Yup. Met a few of the guys there for coffee this morning. Let's go," he said, turning and starting to walk toward his truck.

I stood right where I was, my feet rooted to the ground, because I couldn't seem to function like a normal human being when he was near me. Glancing back to me, Ward nudged his chin in the direction of his truck.

"I'll meet you there," I said quickly.

Right on girl. Look at you! You can still talk.

I really, really didn't appreciate how off-kilter I was around him.

"I'll drop you off later," he replied without hesitation.

His words came out as a statement rather than a question. It was clear he had no expectation I would question him. Normally, I would. He was high handed and a little too domineering for me.

Except in bed.

That was my naughty side. Just as I started to feebly debate that point in my own head, my feet started walking in his direction. My brain was clearly not the driver in this equation.

Ward, of course, had a black truck with every feature you could imagine. It suited him perfectly. The short ride from the station to Firehouse Café was quiet, the air in the truck cab charged. I was wrestling with my desire, struggling to pin it down and vanquish it by my sensible self. Despite my best efforts, it appeared to be a losing cause.

There was that small problem and then the fact I sat there beside him carrying a secret, a very big secret.

When we pulled up at Firehouse Café, I started to climb out on my own, but he moved like lightning. Before I knew it, he was at my door opening it, the momentum from my motion completely stolen by his.

"I could've gotten that, you know," I said, glancing up to catch his eyes.

His lips quirked, a gleam entering his eyes. "I know," he said simply.

We walked across the parking lot, and somewhere along the way, his hand landed on my low back, the heat of his touch like a brand. Ward had the strangest effect on me. I wouldn't have normally described myself as a woman who wanted a man to take care of me. But Ward made me yearn for that. The simple gesture, his hand on my back, made me feel as if I was contained in a circle of his, and his alone.

I wanted to punch back at that feeling and tell it to stop being ridiculous. Sweet hell. I had so many internal battles going on, I had a thunderstorm inside of my own brain. If only Ward knew. He would think I was ridiculous.

I *knew* I was ridiculous.

Chapter Six
SUSANNAH

The cheery bell jingled above the door as Ward opened it, holding it open and gesturing me through. The familiarity of the space eased the jumble of tension in my thoughts. Firehouse Café had been around as long as I could remember. I glanced around as we walked in, reflexively checking to see if anyone I knew was here. Not that it would be particularly inappropriate for me to be seen with Ward. Spending time with any one of the guys on my crew would be perfectly normal.

Yet, I felt restless inside, anxious my attraction to him would somehow be blatantly obvious to anyone who knew me. I breathed a sigh of relief when I saw no one other than Janet James, the owner of the café and a close friend of my parents. She was busy waiting on customers at the counter. There were a few passing acquaintances at the tables, but no one close to me. My tension eased slightly.

Ward started to approach the counter, but I nudged him with my elbow. "Someone will come take our order if we grab a table," I explained.

He nodded and followed me as I aimed straight for a

table in the far back corner. Firehouse Café was aptly named as it was housed in the original fire station for Willow Brook. The original garage had been renovated into a warm and inviting café with an open kitchen and dining counter to one side and tables to the other. Janet had stained the old concrete floor a soft blue color and had rugs scattered about amongst the tables. The space was decorated brightly with painted fireweed flowers on the pole from the upper quarters and artwork from local artists on the walls. The space had a cheerful, relaxed feel to it.

I sat down in the corner, shrugging my jacket off my shoulders and glancing over to Ward as he slipped into the chair across from me. A factor I hadn't considered when I suggested this place was how small the tables were. As I shifted in my chair, my knees bumped into his. That subtle, glancing touch sent a hot jolt through me. I looked over, about to reflexively apologize, and my mouth went dry. He was maybe two feet away across the table, his smoky gaze locked to mine.

Ward was not a man who had a problem with direct eye contact. I had to look away, if only because I was getting hot all over and could feel my cheeks flushing. I almost sighed out loud in relief when Janet approached our table.

"Hey there, Zanna," she said, using a nickname only she and a few other friends and family members called me.

I glanced up with a smile, meeting her bright brown eyes. She had a warm, motherly air to her, although she wasn't a soft person. She'd been running this place on her own for years after her husband died. She had nerves of steel and was resourceful as hell. She also had a heart gigantic enough to encompass just about the whole world.

Her eyes flicked from me to Ward. "Well hello there, Ward. Nice to see you again."

He nodded, a slight smile tugging at one corner of his mouth. Janet was rather irresistible. If anyone could nudge Ward out of being his usual reserved self, Janet could. It wasn't as though that was what she set out to do, it was simply the effect she had on everyone.

"I hope you're settling in nicely here," she added.

Ward's smile stretched to the other corner of his mouth, sending my belly into a tailspin of flutters.

"So far, so good," he commented. His eyes bounced to me. "So Zanna?" he asked, a gleam in his eyes.

Janet chuckled, and I threw an eye roll in her direction. "That's Janet's nickname for me. Not many people use it," I offered.

Ward's eyes didn't lose their glint, and I sensed he would be using that nickname. A little flash of heat scored through me. Only people close to me used that name. I didn't know what to think.

I'd tucked Ward away in a compartment in my mind. Even though I'd been quite intimate with him, I never thought I'd see him again. Even though I could never forget that one night. To have him here, colliding with my world on levels I'd never considered... Well, it was disconcerting to say the least.

I was relieved to have Janet carry on asking Ward a few questions about settling into Willow Brook. I knew how perceptive she was, so it was unlikely she missed the tension between Ward and me. After checking in, she got right to business. "What'll it be tonight?"

"I'll take a salmon burger and sweet potato fries. Do you want to see a menu?" I asked, catching Ward's eyes.

"No need. I'll take the same. Sounds good to me."

"Anything to drink?" Janet asked.

For a second, I was about to order a glass of wine and then remembered I was pregnant. Oh my God. I didn't mind not having a glass of wine, but I was so out of my realm. "No thanks. Just water for me."

Ward eyed me. "You sure?"

"Oh yeah. Long day, and I'm thirsty."

He ordered a beer, and Janet moved along when someone

called her name. He leaned back in his chair, resting one hand on his thigh and an elbow hooked over the back of his chair.

My eyes were drawn to his hand dangling off the chair. Even relaxed, he exuded strength. His hands carried a few scars. As my eyes tracked their way up across the muscled planes of his chest and his shoulders, I couldn't help but notice his clothes did practically nothing to hide his form. My memory of his body was fresh—of how he felt, every inch of him honed by the hard life and rugged strength required of him as a hotshot firefighter.

My eyes landed on his, at which point I blushed from head to toe. He had that heated look in his gaze again, his eyes considering. What he said next startled me.

"I lied."

"Huh?" was my brilliant response.

His lips quirked, his eyes glinting again and sending my belly into another little tizzy.

I scrambled and forced myself to be somewhat coherent. "About what?"

Wow. I managed two complete words this time.

"Saying I'd forget that first night ever happened and then the next one. I can't and I won't," he said bluntly, his gaze sliding down from my face over my breasts and back up.

He might as well have touched me. My nipples puckered tight to an ache almost instantly at the burn from his gaze. A waiter conveniently stopped by to deliver my water and Ward's beer at that moment. I grabbed it and gulped the water down immediately before handing it back. "I could use a refill."

The waiter, a high school kid, gave me a wide-eyed look, but he was quick to recover. He lifted the pitcher of water on his tray and refilled my glass quickly. "Anything else?" he asked.

At the shake of my head, he left, promising to bring our food as soon as it was ready. Ward's gaze had never left me, and I felt hot all over. I took another sip of my water, this time somewhat controlled, and set it down. "Well, you're going to have to forget about it," I finally said.

The intensity of Ward's gaze deepened as he shook his head slowly. "I don't have to do anything." He took a drag of his beer as he considered me. "Why are you lying?"

"I'm not lying."

"You're acting like you can forget about it. I don't believe you," he said flatly.

Okay, I didn't really know where Ward was going with this, but if we were going to have a face the truth moment, I figured I might as well get with the program fast. I took a deep breath and blurted out the truth.

"I'm pregnant."

I couldn't say I was pleased, but at least for once, I had actually shaken Ward's composure. His eyes widened and his head actually went back a little, almost as if I'd punched him verbally.

He gave his head a little shake, his eyes narrowing. "What?" he asked, that single word crisp and clear.

My cheeks were hot, but I doubled down. I didn't back down once I was halfway through something. I was a rip-the-band-aid-off kind of girl. "Just what I said. I'm pregnant."

He took a drag on his beer, guzzling almost half of it. Setting it down with careful deliberation, his hand still curled around it, he cocked his head to the side. "I'm guessing you're going to tell me I'm the only man you've been with in the last month or so."

Anger flashed inside. "Look, I don't know what the hell you think of me, but I don't usually do what I did with you. In fact, you're the only man I've ever just..." My words sputtered.

"Fucked so hard we almost set each other on fire," he offered grimly.

His words sent another flash of heat through me, this

one desire. It collided with my anger like gas to a flame. I took a deep breath, trying to gather myself inside.

"I'm not seeing anyone, and you're the only man I've had sex with in the last year." I paused, annoyed I'd let it slip how little sex there was in my life. But hell, this was already a hot mess, so I'd have to get over it. "There's only one man who could be the father, and it's you. Don't go blaming this on me. We used protection."

"Damn straight. I know we did," he said flatly. "What the fuck happened?"

I was relieved he didn't cling to the idea I might've been with someone else. He seemed to have moved past it quickly, but then Ward was a no bullshit kind of guy.

I leaned my elbows on the table, running my hands through my hair and then resting my chin on one hand and twirling a loose lock of hair around my finger.

"Well, nothing is one-hundred percent, except not having sex," I offered.

Ward took another drag of his beer, his gaze somber as he nodded slowly. I didn't know what I'd expected, but I'd been prepared for him to tell me to fuck off. Not that I had any basis for that expectation. He seemed shocked, but he didn't seem angry, and for that, I was relieved.

Chapter Seven
WARD

The light glinted off one of Susannah's curls—that glorious strawberry blonde hair—as she twirled it around one of her fingers. She traced swirls with another fingertip in the damp moisture on her water glass.

I took another long drag from my beer. She was so fucking gorgeous. Staring into her wide blue eyes, I recalled how hazy and dark they were when she was in the throes of going wild in my arms. My cock twitched.

This was ridiculous. Here I was getting hard over a woman who just told me she was pregnant. What. The. Fuck.

I scrambled for some sanity. I was stunned. I was a damn Boy Scout about using condoms, always prepared. Hell, I'd never even had unprotected sex. Not once. Ever.

Even when I was a teenager, I'd been responsible. I might not have thought it through much, but I damn well knew it was important not to have unprotected sex. So I hadn't, and it didn't even fucking matter in the end.

Susannah was pregnant.

It was obvious she was anxious about telling me this. Hell, she should've been. No matter what I thought, I didn't think she had planned this. She looked as rattled as I felt. She'd been just as dedicated to making sure I got those condoms on too.

I knew there were no guarantees in life, certainly not in sex. This was definitely not something I had ever expected to be dealing with though.

As I stared at Susannah, contemplating what the hell to say, our waiter arrived with our food, setting the plates in front of us. "Need anything else?" he asked.

"Another beer, please," I said.

"Be right back," he replied before spinning away.

Susannah appeared to be waiting for me to say something. I hadn't said much since her explosive announcement. An image flashed in my mind – Susannah pregnant, her belly round, and her breasts—her perfect plump breasts with dusky pink nipples—even fuller than they already were.

Damn. My cock hardened at the thought. What the hell was I thinking?

"Do you want to talk about it?" Susannah finally asked, clearing her throat when her voice got gravelly.

I tried to think of how to talk about this, but I was stumped. "I don't know what the hell to say, so maybe we should just eat right now."

She looked at me for a long moment, her brow furrowing. "I'm sorry."

"For what?"

"Well, I mean, I know you didn't plan on me getting pregnant."

"Just like I know you didn't plan on getting pregnant," I countered.

My level tone belied the confusion spinning in my mind, but at the moment, I didn't think I could think through the jumble, so I focused on the concrete.

A look of relief crossed her face and her shoulders went with a sigh. "No, no I didn't," she said softly.

Our waiter arrived again, taking my empty bottle and handing me a fresh beer. I took a swig, setting it down and holding her gaze. I might not know what the hell to say just now, but if she wanted to talk, I'd try to muddle through. "If you want to talk..."

Her lips quirked as she shrugged. "It's okay. It's as much of a shock to me as you. I've had a few weeks to get used to the idea."

At that, she lifted her burger and took a bite. I followed suit, quickly discovering that the casual dinner fare here was incredible. The salmon burger was glazed with maple syrup and honey mustard. It was obscenely delicious.

Janet, who I'd now met a whopping two times, joined us for a bit. She basically interviewed me about my entire life up to this point. If I hadn't considered it before, I was coming to learn people here had no hesitation at barging into my life. She eventually meandered away, squeezing my shoulder and all but ordering me to stop for coffee every day.

"You'd better get used to that," Susannah said as she pushed her empty plate away after Janet left.

"I can see that. I grew up outside Bozeman, Montana. It's much bigger now, but when I was growing up, it had a small town vibe. I'm used to people being all up in my business," I offered with a shrug.

Curiosity flickered in her gaze, her brows rising slightly. The moment passed, but I realized that this baby—!—meant I might have a shot at something I'd never had. My mother had been the only person I could truly count as family, and she'd been there in every way possible. But the rest—my absentee father, my greedy stepfather and my resentful brother—I could have done without them. Maybe I couldn't recreate my own past, but I could build my own future. I skipped past that train of thought, not ready to contemplate those implications just yet.

After we finished eating, we returned to my truck, and I let Susannah in. After I got in on the driver's side, she glanced my way. "You're quite the gentleman, Ward."

I met her gaze, arching a brow.

"Getting the door for me. Not a lot of men do that these days," she explained.

As I stared at her, I was again envisioning her pregnant. A sense of protectiveness and concern that I had *never* experienced in my life caught me in its grip.

I tore my eyes away with a shrug. "Habit. It's called manners."

I started the truck up and drove away. Without thinking, I started driving to my place rather than returning her to her car at the station.

After a moment, she spoke. "Are you taking me back to my car?"

Hell no.

I couldn't be near Susannah without wanting to be buried inside of her. I'd thought my attraction to her during our training together would fade. Not so. I was in worse shape now than I'd been back then. All I could think was I didn't need to worry about protection and how that meant I could be as close as physically possible to Susannah. I didn't even look her way. Shifting in my seat, I adjusted my jeans with one hand to deal with the aching ridge of my cock.

"Let's go to my place," was all I finally said.

"Should we maybe talk?"

"Well you told me what's going on, and I appreciate that. We have plenty of time to talk. None of that changes what I want and what I know you want," I said flatly.

Her breath drew in sharply. I flicked my eyes to her, a wave of satisfaction rolling through me at the sight of her cheeks flushing.

Reaching across the console between us, I dragged my palm along her thigh, nudging her knees apart and cupping my hand over her mound. I almost groaned at the feel of her damp heat through her jeans. When I exerted subtle pressure just over her clit, she gasped and her hips arched into my touch.

It was hard to imagine she wanted this as much as I did, but our bodies seemed capable of having an entire conversation without a word being spoken. As it was, we didn't say much else.

"All you have to do is say the word if you don't want this," I murmured, flicking my eyes to hers again, my attention half on the road in front of me.

The flush on her cheeks deepened, and her eyes met mine, the blue darkening. She said nothing.

"I'll take that as a yes then," I said as I dragged my thumb back and forth across the fabric above her clit. With each pass, her hips flexed into my palm.

I kept my attention ahead now, absorbing our surroundings as I drove. Willow Brook was in the foothills of the Alaskan Range with the mountains in the distance one way and the ocean another. There were fields of green grasses mingled amongst swaths of spruce forest.

I'd bought a place here before my mom passed away. I hated renting, and there was plenty of property up here with views so spectacular it bordered on ridiculous. I found a nice chunk of property a few miles outside of downtown Willow Brook with a gorgeous timber frame home. It had more space than I needed, but I liked it. Rolling to a stop in front of the house, I finally removed my hand from between Susannah's thighs, instantly missing the heat of her.

Holding the door for her, I watched as she climbed out, my body wracked with need. Kicking the door shut with my boot, I curled my hand around hers and strode quickly inside. I meant to yank her to me the moment we walked in the door because I was that fucking desperate.

For her.

I was a bit of a mess inside, a clusterfuck in my mind. Susannah was pregnant. With my baby. Something I definitely hadn't planned on. I had all kinds of feelings about it, but rising through the scrum of confusion and uncertainty was one word, flashing like neon in my mind whenever I was near her.

Mine.

Chapter Eight
WARD

When we stepped through the side door into my home, Susannah tugged her hand free of mine, much to my chagrin. What I had in mind didn't involve social niceties.

Oblivious to my urge to throw her over my shoulder and cart her to bed, Susannah spun in a circle as she glanced around the downstairs of my home. It was a single level, timber frame ranch style home with a tall ceiling that rose up to a point in the center of the living room and windows across the entire front wall. It was still light out. The days could feel like forever here once winter had passed. Even though it was only spring, the sun wasn't setting until after nine in the evening.

The side door came from a deck into the kitchen, which had soft green tiles and a curved counter that arched off the wall and served as a divider between the kitchen and dining room. Rich, cherry wood cabinets were mounted on the walls with stainless steel appliances. The tile met hardwood flooring beyond the counter. A dining area that phased into the living room was just beyond that. A small round table and chairs furnished the dining area with the back of a sectional couch creating a natural divider for the living room.

One part of the couch faced the wall where a television was mounted and the other side of the couch faced the windows, looking out over the view. A propane fireplace occupied the far corner of the living room. The space was bright and airy. Even though there were three bedrooms, it didn't feel too large for just me.

Although I didn't know if I'd be here beyond the two years for my contract, the price was good, the property was gorgeous, and I figured I could sell if I didn't decide to stay longer.

Susannah spun back to me as she walked backwards into the living room. "This is lovely. You bought this?"

I slid my hands into my pockets, if anything to calm the restless urge to snatch her to me and devour her. "I did."

She nodded as she turned away, walking towards the windows. Resting one hand on her hip, she looked out. The view faced a sloping hill with a cluster of cottonwood trees to one side and a rocky hillside to the other. A valley beyond was barely visible in the fading light. The sky was streaked with orange and red, the lingering burst from the setting sun.

"Beautiful view," she commented. "My friends built this home, but I never got to see the inside after it was finished."

Turning back, she walked toward where I had stopped beside the couch, resting a hip against the back of it.

"Oh?"

"Have you met Amelia? Cade's wife?" she asked.

"Think so. She's tall, right?"

Susannah's lips quirked. "Yeah, she's tall. She owns and runs Kick Ass Construction with Lucy. They're good friends of mine. Anyway, they run one of the best construction companies in town. They built this house only a few years ago if I remember right. I can't believe the owners sold it so quickly, but they were out-of-towners anyway."

I chuckled. "This is definitely a small town if you know who used to own this place."

Her eyes flicked to mine and she nodded. "Well, yeah. But I probably wouldn't have known who had this place if Amelia and Lucy hadn't built it."

She had stopped a few feet away from me. The urge to touch her was too powerful to resist anymore. I reached out, catching her hand in mine and reeling her to me. Snagging her bottom lip in her teeth, her cheeks pinkened as she looked up at me. Fuck me. The sight of her teeth denting her plump lip sent blood shooting to my groin.

I leaned my hips against the back of the sofa, pulling her between my knees. Her breath hissed through her teeth when her hips bumped into the ridge of my cock. I didn't bother to hide my arousal. There was no point to it. I'd been hanging onto my control by a thread all evening.

Her brow furrowed as she held my gaze. I could tell she was thinking. I wasn't in denial. I knew we had plenty to talk about. I just didn't feel like talking right now. I'd rather lose myself in her for a bit.

As if she could read my mind, she asked, "Shouldn't we talk?"

I shrugged, letting my hand slide around her hips to cup her bottom. Damn. She had a sweet ass. "Maybe," I replied, as I slid my other hand under the hem of her shirt, almost groaning at the feel of her silky soft skin.

I hadn't thought about it much, but something about how she was such a tomboy on the outside and so feminine on the inside drove me crazy. I respected the hell out of her. I knew she could hold her own with any man out in the field. Word amongst the crew here was she was fearless, and it wasn't as if I hadn't known that. I'd seen her in action when we trained together. I loved her strength and her reckless edge. It was impossible to do the job we did without it. Our job required a tolerance for danger, for pushing past the point where most would turn back.

Her breath hitched, distracting me. My eyes wandered down over the swell of her breasts. She wore jeans and a T-shirt. There was nothing whatsoever remarkable about her outfit. Yet, she was sexy as hell. She had a penchant for lace and silk, something I'd discovered in our two nights together. Her nipples pressed against the cotton of her T-shirt, her breasts stretching the fabric tight.

I dipped my head, nipping through her T-shirt over a nipple, savoring the sharp gasp from her and the instant rock of her hips into mine.

"Ward," she murmured when I pinched her other nipple between my thumb and forefinger.

Lifting my head, I canted my eyes up to meet hers, level with mine since I was halfway seated. "Yes?" I managed.

"You didn't answer me."

For a flash, I wasn't catching her meaning, then I recalled her question. "I don't think we have to talk now, do we?"

Her breast rose into my palm as she took a shuddering breath. "Well, I don't know."

Little furrows appeared between her brows, her teeth catching her lip again. I doubted she meant for that to be a turn on, but it was sexy as all hell. Her mouth alone could bring me to my knees. Those plump pink lips, the fair skin of her face and her wide blue eyes. I remembered those lips wrapped around my cock and couldn't wait to see it again.

I realized she was going to be stuck in this place if I didn't give her a chance to talk. I had to force myself to focus. The need roaring through me was like a river rushing down a mountain. I could hardly hear over it as it pushed everything else out of the way.

"Look, I get it. I know we need to talk. You're pregnant. I'm shocked about it, but I don't know that we're going to solve anything tonight. I need a little time to get used to the idea, and I don't know what you want to do. Do you?"

She held my gaze, shifting on her feet. "Obviously, I didn't plan on this. I wasn't sure if I wanted a baby, but I can't imagine anything else. But..." She paused and took a slow breath. "I think you're right. I think we need a little time to absorb it."

I stared at her—hard. I was still too startled by the news to know what to say. But I did know one thing. I wanted her. Now.

Chapter Nine
WARD

Susannah shifted on her feet again, worrying her bottom lip with her teeth. "You're technically my boss now. We have to figure this out. It's more than just the baby."

I knew she was right, but I'd already done some thinking. Right now, I was perfectly content to have this be nobody's business but ours.

"We'll figure it out," I said.

I had no idea what we would do. I had my doubts we could keep this on the casual level, not with a baby factored into the equation. In fact, the odd thing was, the direction I was going inside would likely scare her off. Hell, it frightened me on its own. Yet, it felt right. If we were going to do this, I wasn't going to do it halfway. No child of mine would get the half of a family I had. I knew I had to play it slow though, if only because I sensed Susannah would push back against me demanding what I wanted. So I'd wait.

Like a drum beating inside my body, the only thing I could act on was the here and now—Susannah in my arms and the need to claim her driving me with such force I couldn't ignore it.

She finally nodded, taking a deep breath and letting it out in a sigh. "Fine. I'll let it go for now."

"Good," I said with a smile tugging at the corners of my lips, dragging my thumb back and forth across her nipple, savoring the feel of it tightening under my touch.

Leaning back slightly, I slid her shirt up and over her head, relieved when she didn't hesitate, lifting her arms. I groaned at the sight of her breasts. She had on this black lace bra, a ridiculous excuse for a bra. Her nipples played peekaboo with me through the lace as I leaned forward, laving my tongue over the silk, swirling around and sucking her nipple into my mouth.

When she was thinking, Susannah was reserved. Yet when she stopped thinking, she just completely let go, and I fucking loved it. Like now. The moment I bit down on her nipple, cupping her other breast in my palm and savoring the heavy weight of it, she cried out and arched into me.

Lifting my head, our mouths collided. Kissing her was like a drug. I devoured her mouth. Her tongue tangling roughly with mine, she gasped into my mouth, murmuring my name into our kiss. All the while, her hands got busy, sliding up under my shirt, coasting over my chest. She cried out when I flicked the clasp between her breasts, growling as they tumbled free into my palms. Her lips were on mine again, her breasts against my skin, and I couldn't get enough of her.

Breaking free from our kiss, I leaned back, taking her in. Her breasts nearly slayed me—plump and round, her nipples puckered tight, already damp from my attentions. I flicked my eyes up to meet her gaze. The bright blue of her eyes darkened to navy. Her lips were damp and puffy, swollen from the roughness of our kiss.

Susannah made me crazy, so crazy I lost sight of what I was doing. Nothing was calculated, everything had a rough, wild edge to it. My cock was so hard, I likely had an imprint from my zipper on it.

She remedied that quickly, reaching between us and tearing my fly open. Her lips curled in a sly grin.

Chapter Ten
SUSANNAH

I sighed at the feel of Ward's cock in my palm—hot and hard, the skin velvety soft. No briefs or boxers, Ward was a commando man. It suited him perfectly. There was nothing civilized about him. He was all raw, primal man, wrapped in a body so damn sexy and so damn hard all over, he stole my breath just by existing.

My heartbeat thundered, pounding through my body like a drum. A sense of power rolled through me at the sound of his ragged groan when I slid my palm up and down his cock. Stepping back, I knelt down between his knees, swirling my tongue around the tip of his cock and catching the drop of pre-cum there. I flicked my gaze up to find his eyes on me, dark and intent. He slid a hand into my hair, the rough edge to his touch akin to striking a match, scattering sparks over my skin and making me hot all over.

Another swirl of my tongue and then I drew him in my mouth, every hard, thick inch of him. Just like the rest of him, his cock was glorious. It pulsed as I drew him into my mouth, letting my palm get wet and gripping him loosely as I slid up and down with my mouth. With a rough tug, he reached for me, lifting me swiftly.

"Hey, I wasn't done," I muttered, my voice husky.

I collided with his smoky gaze. He shrugged. "Can't wait," he growled.

In a matter of seconds, he was shoving my jeans and panties down. Before I could form a thought, he was stretching me out on the couch, every inch of me bare to his heated gaze. Leaning up, I yanked at the hem of his T-shirt.

"This needs to come off," I demanded.

He grinned, his eyes flashing. Reaching behind his neck, he lifted his shirt up and over in one fell swoop. He stood before me as my eyes greedily soaked him up. His chest was all muscle, a dusting of dark hair on it. His jeans hung open at his hips, his cock still damp from my mouth.

Ward was utterly un-self conscious. Not that there was any reason whatsoever for him to be self-conscious. He was a specimen of beauty, every inch of him honed to hardness, so damn sexy and so damn glorious. My mouth went dry just looking at him.

He shoved his jeans down, kicking them free along with his boots. He leaned over me, trailing his fingertips down across my breasts, the subtle touch sending hot shivers through me. He meandered down over my belly, pausing just above the apex of my thighs, his eyes on me the entire time.

I would have done anything he said just now. That was how bad it was. I was a slave to the need between us and to the power he exuded.

Without a word, his gaze searing into me, his fingers slipped through my curls and dipped into my core. I moaned. Hot and slick, I was so needy for him I was beside myself. His knee sank onto the couch between my thighs, nudging them apart slightly. He sank one finger inside of me, knuckle deep. A ragged moan escaped my lips. Another finger joined the first. My hips rolled into his touch as he fucked me with his fingers.

"I want to watch you come apart right now, to come all over my hand," he murmured, his words rough, making my pulse pound even harder and sending hot shivers through me.

Even his voice was a turn on for me, every word he uttered making me wild with need inside.

"More than that though, I want to feel you come all over my cock."

His silver-smoke gaze held mine as he drew his fingers out and sank them inside again. I cried out, my pussy clenching. I was already on the edge when he teased across my clit, just enough pressure to push me a little closer to the edge but not enough to take me over.

He curled his fist around his cock, stroking it lightly as his fingers drove me wild. Hunger coiled inside as I saw another drop of pre-cum roll out, glistening on the tip before it dripped onto my belly.

"I suppose we should discuss protection," he said, his words nudging my eyes back to his. "Since you're pregnant, we don't have to worry about that, but I don't know how you feel about it. I'm clean. I've never in my life had sex without a condom."

"Me neither," I murmured, this conversation feeling suddenly intimate.

"So?" he drawled. "Your call."

The idea of Ward being bare inside of me made me hot all over. That was saying something since I was practically on fire already. I swallowed. "There's no need."

He held my gaze, sliding his fist up and down his cock as he stared at me. Without a word, he slowly withdrew his fingers from where they'd been buried inside of me. Levering over me slightly, he dragged the thick head of his cock through my folds. I was dripping wet with need. With every pass, his cock slid across my clit, nearly pushing me over the edge.

"You want this, don't you?" he murmured, teasing me relentlessly. "You're so fucking wet."

"Ward, please..." My voice came out in a ragged, breathy plea.

"Look at me."

My eyes slammed into his, the look there alone tightening the pressure gathering inside of me. With his eyes locked to mine, he dragged his cock over my clit again as my hips bucked into him.

"Please," I begged.

I didn't even recognize myself. Ward turned me into a mess of need and desperation, nothing but desire driving me. Desire for him to claim me, to bury his cock inside of me and fuck me so hard, I might, maybe just for a few moments, be satiated.

He didn't rush. Oh no. With his smoky gaze locked to mine, he dragged the head of his cock through my slick folds again, teasing my entrance and then passing up over my clit, sending yet another spike of pleasure shooting through me. I cried out and only then did he sink inside. In one swift surge, he filled me completely.

I was teetering on the edge of detonation already, my nerves so sensitized, it bordered on painful. Ward held still inside of me, his gaze locked to mine, searing me with its intensity. It felt so good to have him bare inside of me, no barrier between us. He drew his hips back slowly before seating himself again, the slide of his cock in my channel sending sparks of heat flying inside.

I couldn't break free from his silver smoky gaze. The intimacy of the moment was shocking. My entire body was vibrating, while my heart thudded hard and fast. He drew back again, this time surging inside quickly and then holding still. He lifted a hand, brushing my tangled hair away from my forehead. I soaked in the feel of him stretching me, bringing me to the brink, pleasure spinning and coiling tighter and tighter. It felt so good to be held within his gaze and encompassed within the sheer power of his presence.

His eyelids started to fall, his words slurred as he spoke. "So fucking good. You feel so good."

My hips arched into him reflexively, the vibration in my body impossible to withstand. The moment I moved, he drew back and finally gave me what I needed—hard and fast, his hips pounding into me.

Every beat of every thrust stretching me and filling me. Never once did his eyes break away. His hand slid down over my breasts, giving a gentle pinch to my nipple before his touch trailed over my belly, his thumb pressing over my clit. Pleasure exploded, shattering into pieces inside of me. I flew apart, lost in the throes of a climax so intense it ruined me.

With my pussy clamping down around his cock, I dimly heard him cry out as his body went rigid and he sank into me once again, the heat of his release filling me. He held still for a beat, his muscles taut as he looked down at me. He slowly eased down, rolling us over so that I rested atop him with his cock still buried inside of me. I lay still, my breath gusting as I felt his heartbeat pounding against my own. His palm slid down my back in a slow pass, coming to rest on the curve of my bottom.

There was something about being held by Ward, even when relaxed he felt so strong. Held tight against him with him buried inside of me, I felt as if nothing could get to me. All of a sudden, it hit me. I was pregnant, and Ward knew.

The moment that thought crossed my mind, I tensed.

"Don't start thinking yet, Zanna," he murmured, his voice a rough whisper above my head.

I flushed to realize he could sense I had started to worry. I laughed softly, the tension easing as I lifted my head, resting my chin on my hand.

Sweet hell. There should be a law against men looking as sexy as he did. With his black curls tousled, the shadow of his beard, his chiseled features and those eyes...fuck me, those eyes. He could seduce a woman with nothing more than a look.

I didn't dare tell him he could probably make me come just by looking at me. I had some pride.

He opened his eyes, a subtle glint in them.

"Well I'm sure you'd agree, we might have something to talk about," I said, feeling bashful all of a sudden.

His hand slid up and down my back in another slow pass, giving my ass cheek a squeeze. He shrugged, his shoulder lifting against me. "I suppose, but we could relax now and talk later."

"Are you going to take me back to my car tonight?" I asked.

He grinned, one of those ridiculous grins that made my belly flip. "No. You're staying."

"That wasn't a question. Were you planning to ask me if I wanted to stay?"

His grin stretched to the other side of his mouth as he shook his head. "No."

"I don't usually take orders," I countered.

He held my gaze, that silver flashing again. "Sometimes you do."

I flushed straight through, recalling our last night together when he ordered me to turn around on the bed and arch my back—because he wanted to see "*your sweet ass and your pussy.*"

I hadn't hesitated. I hadn't even questioned it. That was only one of several times he ordered me around that night.

I rolled my eyes, trying to keep my composure. "Fine. Sometimes I do."

I didn't really want to leave tonight. The idea of curling up beside him and falling asleep, well, that would be heaven.

He didn't give me much of a chance to contemplate this. He shifted to slide out from under me, lifting me into his arms from the couch. In a matter of seconds, he was carrying me into the shower. With the water running down over us and steam cocooning us, I was rinsing the water out of my eyes when I heard his palm land on the tile wall beside me. His other palm slapped on the other side, and I stood in a cage of his arms. With his curls damp and water running in rivulets down his magnificent body, my channel clenched.

"So let's make one thing clear," he said.

"What's that?"

"You're mine."

The following morning, I insisted Ward drop me off at my car early. I didn't want to run the risk of anyone from the crew noticing us arriving at the station together. He hadn't offered much on the point, but had gone along with it. Afterwards, I drove over to grab some coffee at Firehouse Café and headed home to change my clothes.

As I got ready to leave again, his words spun through my thoughts again. *You're mine.*

What the hell? I didn't even know what to think about that. I was annoyed with the part of me that savored his streak of possessiveness. I mean, good grief. I wasn't the kind of woman who needed a man to take care of her. While I couldn't deny the force of my attraction to Ward—even I knew that was pointless—I was starting to think it had to be hormones. Dr. Jenkins had warned me to be prepared for the influx of hormonal changes, which would affect me in a range of ways. So this crazy, out of control desire must be that. I'd let it ride, but I wasn't about to let him think he had a claim to me just because I was pregnant and he happened to be the father.

The more I thought about it, the more apparent it became I needed to keep my boundaries clear. Otherwise, he'd dominate his way right into my life.

Chapter Eleven
WARD

The following day, I strolled into the front area of the station and found Beck leaning on the counter, laughing at something. Maisie's cheeks were flushed as she glanced my way.

"Hey Ward," Maisie said, brushing a curl out of her eyes. "Do you need anything?"

"Rumor has it you handle ordering supplies," I said.

"She sure does. You'll have better luck than me. She's too worried about making sure she doesn't treat me special around here," Beck offered with a sly grin.

Maisie threw a pen at him, which Beck caught easily. Their banter was so easy-going, the love between them clear. Because I had it that bad for Susannah, it crossed my mind it was convenient for me to know there were interoffice relationships around here. If there was such a thing as an office when it came to being a hotshot firefighter.

With a roll of her eyes at Beck, Maisie glanced back to me. "Just let me know what you need. I do orders every Monday. I handle all the office supplies plus the crew equipment."

"Got it. Things look pretty good so far, but I had a few requests, so thought I'd check."

Maisie nodded, her curls bouncing with the motion. "Just let me know. Oh, and ignore Beck. He gets treated just the same as all of you here."

Beck pushed away from the counter, flashing her another grin. "Exactly the problem. I give you foot rubs every night, and I get nothing special for it."

Maisie's phone rang. She threw a glare and a kiss Beck's way before taking the call and shooing us away.

Beck walked with me into the back hallway. There were a few offices along the hall and then it opened up into a massive break room with a kitchen, a pool table, a television and a work out room off to one side, along with a few bedrooms. From what I gathered, most of the guys on the crew lived here locally, but some flew in only for fire season and stayed at the station.

As we rounded the corner into the break room area, the hair on the back of my neck rose. I knew without seeing her that Susannah was here. There were a few guys lounging on the couch in front of the television, while Susannah stood at the kitchen counter filling a tea kettle with water. She glanced over her shoulder as Beck and I came into the room.

The moment her eyes landed on mine, they widened and a flush crested on her cheeks. Seeing her was a jolt to my system, a straight shot of lust in my veins.

Her strawberry blonde curls were tamed into a ponytail. A few curls had fallen loose, dangling along her cheeks. She wore jeans with boots and a T-shirt. My eyes, my greedy eyes, willfully flicked down and then back up. Her nipples were taut, pressing against the cotton of her shirt.

My mind flashed back to the other night—her nipples damp from my mouth, her channel clenching around me as I pounded into her. The recollection was so sharp, blood shot straight to my groin.

She looked away, abruptly setting the kettle on the stove

and then clicking on the burner before turning around and crossing her arms. "Hi guys. How's it going?" she asked politely.

Beck leaned against the counter beside Susannah, hopefully oblivious to the tension between her and me.

He nudged her with his elbow. "Be nice to Ward. He's still getting used to things here."

Susannah glanced from him to me, rolling her eyes as her gaze returned to him. "Beck, I'm pretty sure Ward can handle himself. He doesn't need me, or anyone, to baby him."

Beck clearly liked to tease, and anyone was fair game. He shrugged easily. "Of course. But still. Be nice."

Someone called Beck's name from the workout room, and he ambled away, leaving Susannah alone with me. I'd been aching for her for a month straight and finally gotten another taste of her. I was beginning to realize I wasn't even close to satiating my need for her.

What I wanted to do was pick her up, cart her out of here and lose myself in her for days. I knew I needed to sort out how to deal with the reality of our situation. She was pregnant, and we were having a baby. I couldn't tell if I was so stunned by those facts that I couldn't face them. All I could think about was what I wanted—the hottest sex this side of the Mississippi, so we should keep having more of it.

I'd been on firefighter crews for four years now. Relationships among crewmembers weren't unusual. On my last crew, another one of the superintendents was married to one of the crewmembers. They'd been in training together and married within their first year of work. Though I couldn't quite imagine myself married, somehow I kept using this example in my mind when I told myself it was perfectly fine for me to lust after Susannah. There was also the small matter of the fact she was carrying my baby, and it made me crazy protective. Well, that and the fact I didn't intend to let her go.

Chapter Twelve
WARD

The following day, I leaned back in my chair at the table in the break room and glanced around. This was a busy station. Given that it housed three crews, that was no surprise. Yet, the size of the town belied the busyness of the station. Since it was a central location in Alaska, it served a number of other areas.

Nursing my coffee, I pondered how and when to handle the issue of Chad. Rex had been spot on with his assessment. The guy was an asshole, his attitude a problem for the team. We'd responded to a local fire in a nearby town this week. There'd been a large fire at a property with a collection of buildings. The sparks from the initial fire ended up setting two sheds on fire. In short, it was a mess. Chad had been negative the entire time. He grudgingly responded to orders from the two foremen on the team, one of which was Susannah.

Although my predecessor might've put off dealing with the issue, Al had left a trail of documentation regarding the problems, setting me up to deal with Chad whenever I wanted. At the moment, I was trying to suss out if anyone on the crew was close to him. I needed to assess if making a quick decision to fire him would shake up the team. I'd been superintendent for my last team in Montana and before that foreman on another crew. Adjusting to new leadership had its challenges under the best of circumstances. Starting off by firing someone wasn't always a good move, even when it was warranted.

A couple of the guys were working out, and a few others lounging in the back of the break room in front of the television. Meanwhile, I sipped coffee and plowed through a few of the online training courses I needed to finish up.

Cade entered the room from the hallway, pausing by the coffee pot and filling a cup before walking over to join me at the table. He ran a hand through his shaggy brown curls, flashing a grin my way as he sat down. "How are you settling in?" he asked.

I tapped save on the screen before closing my laptop. "All in all, doing okay. I got everything moved in last month when I came up." I was relieved we'd already gotten through the niceties about my mother passing away.

He nodded, sipping his coffee. "Rumor has it you bought the place out on Fireweed Lane."

"Rumor would be right. I heard your wife built it. Damn nice place."

Cade grinned. "That she did. Amelia's one of the best builders in town."

"Yeah. I love it. That's why I bought it. The price was right too."

Cade's resemblance to his father was impossible to miss. In that vein, I commented, "Mind sharing the station with your dad?"

He chuckled, shaking his head with a wry grin. "Nah. When I was a teen, it wasn't so great to have my dad as the police chief, but I grew up. Now we can keep tabs on each other, but we don't really step on each other's toes."

"Good to know," I said with a chuckle. Considering Cade

had been filling in with Beck to manage my crew until I started, I figured it was worth asking for his feedback on Chad. He might have more insight and knowledge on how the crew felt about Chad.

"Speaking of your dad, he gave me a heads up on Chad. Any thoughts on that situation?"

Cade took a healthy swig of his coffee. "Probably not much more than my dad gave you. I would say it's best to deal with him sooner rather than later. There's no love lost between him and anyone on the crew."

"I'm trying to weigh whether to take care of it soon, or wait a bit for the team to get to know me. No matter what, it doesn't set a good precedent for the new boss to show up and fire someone."

Cade leaned back in his chair and let out a sigh, his gaze considering. "Good point. But I don't know if it's worth the wait. He's so pissed he didn't even get an interview for the position, it's just made his attitude worse. I'd be worried about the effect he has on morale."

I gulped my coffee, setting it down and idly tracing circles around the bottom of my mug. "Fair point. Well, Al's got a wall of documentation about disciplinary issues with him. I might just go ahead and act on it. With you and Beck covering for me last month, any thoughts on whether it would be good to have one or both of you sit in with me on this conversation with him?"

Cade nodded slowly. "Good idea. We've both been here a while, so the crew trusts us. Beck's been here longer than me. Us being a part of the decision will take the pressure off of you. We've got your back one-hundred percent, so does Rex and probably the team."

I'd already developed a healthy respect for Cade and Beck. They were rock solid and had the respect of everybody in the station with the exception of Chad, but then Chad didn't appear to grasp the concept of respect. Neither one of them threw their weight around much though. They earned genuine respect, rather than trying to demand it.

"Well let's plan on it sometime in the next few days."

"Sounds like a plan. Be good to take care of it before next week. My crew's scheduled for a training then."

"Got it. How about the day after tomorrow?"

At that moment, Chad returned from the workout area, walking through the break room. His gaze was flat without a spark of friendliness as he scanned the room. He greeted no one, simply walking past us and heading for the showers.

Cade quickly changed the subject. "Anytime you want me to take you out for some fishing this summer, just let me know. I grew up here, so I know all the good spots."

Before I'd known Susannah was stationed here, one of my attractions to the area was the fishing and hunting. Montana had plenty, but Alaska was another level. The wilderness here was so massive, the opportunities seemed endless.

That evening, Beck invited me to join them at Wildlands. As I left the station to meet them there, I couldn't help but wonder if Susannah would be there. It had been a full three nights since our night together. She'd been avoiding me since then, and I wasn't pleased. In fact, I was restless and frustrated in more ways than one.

I could hardly bear to see her around the station without wanting to lay claim to her. Meanwhile, she was doing her damnedest to pretend like there was nothing between us. My original decision to let this be our business was proving to be problematic. We needed to talk soon. I needed her. Soon.

A short drive later, I rolled to a stop in front of Wildlands, glancing around. The lodge sat on the shores of Swan Lake, a picturesque lake, large and sprawling in the center of

Willow Brook. Wildlands was by far the largest lodge on the lake's shores, yet there were others circling the edges of the lake. Several docks for floatplanes were scattered on the shores as well. The lake was gorgeous with a stunning view of the mountains in the distance. The namesake for the lake, the elegant trumpeter swans, floated serenely on the water's surface.

Pocketing my keys, I strolled in the back door from the parking lot, pushing into the hallway. As I passed through, I couldn't help but remember my kiss with Susannah here a month ago. The effects of that night were reverberating in my life in ways I couldn't have predicted.

My mind flashed to the other night, to the feel of her channel clenching down around my cock as I sank into her—the hottest, most intense release of my life.

I shook my head, trying to knock those thoughts out of my mind. I didn't seem capable of even thinking about Susannah without getting hard. This was a problem I'd never dealt with. Control wasn't an issue for me. Yet, Susannah made a mockery of my control by her sheer existence.

Entering the restaurant, I threaded through the tables, joining Cade, Beck, Levi, and a few others. They'd commandeered a large round table in a back corner. Conversation meandered along while I nursed a beer, listened to the guys joke and wondered the entire time if and when Susannah would make an appearance. She made me wait just long enough to get cranky.

The hair on the back of my neck prickled, my body's knowledge of her presence cueing me before I even saw her. Glancing over my shoulder, I saw her walking across the restaurant. Her eyes met mine, and lust lashed at me. My cock was hard instantly, so hard, I had to shift in my seat and adjust my jeans.

Conveniently, there was only one open seat at the table, right beside me. Amelia was here with Cade, Maisie with Beck, and Lucy with Levi. The urge to publicly claim

Susannah was so strong, yet I knew I needed to check that urge. I knew she wouldn't appreciate it, not now. This was a problem I had to solve sooner rather than later.

She slipped into the chair beside me, her eyes flicking up to mine. Glancing down to her, my heart gave a hard thump. My mind was doing crazy things. While I could hardly think logically about the fact she was pregnant, I had no trouble conjuring images of her full and pregnant with our baby.

Chapter Thirteen
SUSANNAH

My pulse lunged, the moment my eyes locked with Ward's. I'd successfully managed to avoid any alone time with him the last few days. It was sheer willpower on my part to avoid him. I was going crazy inside, literally at battle with myself.

I wanted him badly, the ferocity of my desire making me feel crazy. I wasn't accustomed to this kind of desire. Sex with him was like a drug.

Hell, I was already addicted. My mind spun back to the other night and what he said.

Mine.

I was a muddled hormonal mess. I was pregnant, planning to have our baby and conflicted about Ward's presence in my life. I didn't want to be forced into this situation with him. But a baby was serious. No matter what. I couldn't exactly shut him out, yet I wanted to keep the boundaries clear and not allow him to think he could take over.

Someone said my name, nudging my thoughts back to reality. I needed to get a grip. Following the direction of the voice, I found Maisie looking at me expectantly.

"Yeah?" I asked.

She giggled, flicking a brown curl off her cheek. "I was just saying hi. We can't stay late tonight, so no cards."

Lucy Caldwell, a blonde haired fairy and close friend, rolled her eyes from across the table. "Oh, that'll be terrible. You won't be here to kick all of our asses."

Maisie shrugged. "Hey, I learned one good thing from my dad, and it was how to kick ass at cards."

Amelia piped up. "Good thing we trust you, or I'd think you counted cards or something."

Maisie's dark brown eyes widened, a look of affront crossing her face. "Don't even say that."

Lucy rolled her eyes. "We know you don't cheat. Get over it."

Conversation carried on around us, and I felt the burn of Ward's gaze on me.

"Stop looking at me like that," I whispered.

He didn't respond, taking a pull from his beer and then sliding his hand onto my thigh under the table, the heat of his touch sending a flash of heat spiraling through me.

I flicked my eyes to him, tearing them away after a second. Because I could hardly bear to look at him without getting drawn into his searing gaze.

"What are you doing?" I hissed.

He squeezed my thigh, his palm sliding up, strong and sure, and coming to rest at the crease by my hip. My attention was drawn to his touch, my pulse throbbing. My sex clenched, and my panties were wet instantly.

He took another drag on his beer, setting it down and replying conversationally to something Beck said. Hell if I knew what. I was so distracted to have Ward beside me and his hand on me, I could hardly think, much less pay attention to anything around me.

I was quite relieved the table was full and everyone was in the swing of chatting, eating, and drinking. When the waiter swung by, I shook my head at the offer of a beer and requested water. The entire time, I felt the heat of Ward's gaze on me, sensing the absence of his attention when he commented on something else someone said.

His touch, stealthy and sure, dragged along that sensitive crease, my pussy practically begging for his touch. He didn't disappoint, his palm cupping over my mound. I swallowed, making a feeble effort to resist the urge to arch into him. I gulped some water and took a shuddering breath. "Stop it!" I hissed, trying to keep my expression calm and never once looking at him.

"Only if you tell me why you've been avoiding me," he answered, sotto voce.

"Because this is crazy," I whispered. "We work together, and frankly, you're my boss." Taking another gulp of water, I wished I could cool off. I could've used a stiff drink about now, but that wasn't an option.

Maisie said something to me, and I glanced her way. Ward took that moment to drag his fingers over my clit, teasing me through the denim of my jeans.

I managed to choke out a response to Maisie. "What was that?"

My capacity to listen was nearly obliterated.

"When was the last time you were up in Fairbanks?" she repeated. If she noticed I was out of it, she let it slide.

"Oh, that was two months ago now," I managed, my voice cracking on the last word.

"Oh, okay," she said, returning to whatever the hell she was talking about with Beck.

"You need to stop," I whispered fiercely, once her attention was off of me.

"No," Ward replied.

I finally flicked my eyes over to his to find his gaze waiting for me. A smile teased at the corners of his mouth. On command, my belly flipped once, twice, and then again, flutters spinning it wild.

"Ward..." I warned

His low chuckle sent a shiver down my spine.

"Come home with me," was his only reply.

Because I was starting to feel like a coward, I finally held his gaze, willing my body to relax and my expression to remain calm. I was relieved for the slightly dim lighting in the bar, hoping my flushed cheeks wouldn't be obvious to anyone looking my way.

"Tonight?"

He nodded slowly, sliding his hand out from where he'd been teasing me, his palm resting easily on my thigh. I instantly missed the heat of his touch between my thighs. Masking my restlessness with another sip of water, I took a breath.

"Yes. Tonight," he said, enunciating clearly

"Look, we can..." My words trailed off when he shook his head sharply.

"Look, I get that you're driving the bus here. It's your body, but you told me you wanted this baby, so I'm adjusting on the fly." He was speaking low enough for no one else to hear, but I had to hold back the urge to glance around just in case. "You said it yourself, we need to talk. I wasn't up for it the other night, but now you've been completely avoiding me for three days straight. Not cool," he said bluntly.

Indignation rose inside with a flash of heat. I narrowed my eyes. "I haven't been avoiding you."

A blatant lie I didn't mind admitting to myself, but I wasn't fessing up to him. His eyes darkened to smoke, his hand sliding stealthily between my thighs again. My hips shifted reflexively into his touch this time, and I had to bite my lip to keep from moaning.

"If I have to play dirty, I will," he said pointedly.

I was a hot mess inside. That was the plain truth. I hadn't expected to get pregnant. I was scrambling on my own to figure out how to adjust to this reality and what it meant for me. I sure as hell hadn't expected to be facing a man who would now be permanently part of our child's life, and as a result, my life.

When his fingers drew away again, my words slipped out unbidden. "I've been avoiding you because we can't just have sex all the time."

I gulped my water again, fighting the flush of heat, wishing the ice water could cool me as quickly as his eyes heated me.

"And why is sex a problem? I don't see anything wrong with it. We're pretty damn good at it. If you think for one hot minute I'm walking away, you'd better think again. I didn't plan on any of this, but it's a part of my life now, so I'm dealing with it. You'd better get ready for me to be a part of your life for a long damn time."

A little thrill raced through me, savoring the raw demand in his words and the heat in his eyes. That was how bad I had it for him.

Hormones, it's just hormones.

That was what I kept telling myself. Maybe if I said it enough, I'd believe it.

Chapter Fourteen
WARD

Susannah made me fucking crazy. I got near her, and I turned into a caveman. I was so discombobulated by the situation, my thoughts were a tangled mess of emotions. I wanted her, like I'd never wanted any woman before. Every encounter between us only seemed to ratchet up the tension inside me, the drum of lust beating faster and faster.

Meanwhile, she was pregnant. I couldn't say I'd contemplated the idea of family, of being a father. Ever.

In fact, had you asked me about it, my answer would've been *hell no*.

Yet, now that I was facing the very real, dead serious fact that I was on the way to being a father? Well, my perspective had shifted in a flash. Once the knowledge of our baby solidified in my mind, I knew what I wanted. I'd make damn sure our baby had the family I'd never had.

Aside from my mother, I hadn't been close to anyone in my family. She'd done her damnedest to be everything to me and my brother. I didn't blame her for one second she'd had the bad luck to stumble into two marriages that hadn't been worth it. That was life. I'd learned something from my absentee father and jerk of a stepfather—everything I didn't want to be.

As a consequence, I was bound and determined to fully be a part of our baby's life. I might not yet be ready to call what I felt for Susannah *love*, but I knew damn well it was more powerful than anything I'd ever felt for any woman.

I stared down into Susannah's wide blue eyes, flashing with anger. I knew she was pissed. In fact, I was quite confident she didn't allow any man to tell her what to do. Yet, this thing she was doing — ignoring me and avoiding me — that wasn't going to continue.

At my blunt words, her eyes narrowed. After a taut moment, the air heavy around us, she looked away and took a gulp of her water.

"Do we have to have this conversation now?" she murmured.

"Not this second. But later. You avoiding me isn't going to fly."

Her eyes darted around the table. I didn't give a damn if she was worried someone might notice us talking. Her tongue swiped across her lips, making my cock, already aching hard, even harder.

Her eyes flicked back to mine, a hint of vulnerability in the depths. "Okay," she said softly. "Promise me you won't make a scene. Why don't you come to my place?"

I bit back the urge to demand she come to mine. But I relented. I'd meet her halfway. "That works. When?"

"Tomorrow?" she hedged.

I shook my head. "No. I'm not waiting to see you any longer."

Her breath hissed as it drew in sharply, her eyes looking away as a flush crested on her cheeks. "You can't just tell me what to do," she muttered.

"That's not what I'm trying to do. I want you. You want me. No sense in denying that. But we're also having a baby. I might not have planned on it, but I'm not walking away. We're going to sort out why the hell you're avoiding me."

She looked away again, but nodded slightly. "Fine. Tonight."

Susannah held firm to her insistence that we go to her place. In the parking lot behind Wildlands, we had a little debate where she again tried to blow me off until a couple of crew members came out, Chad included, and the obvious occurred to her. Either we met somewhere privately, or this conversation, which I doubt she wanted anyone to witness, might be observed by others.

I followed her out to her place, rolling to a stop beside her car. It was late evening, going on nine o'clock. The sun was setting, the sky a watercolor of pinks and purples shot through with gold. The moon was rising behind the mountains in the distance. Climbing out of my truck, I watched as an eagle flew above us, a dark shadow against the sky.

Susannah stepped out, glancing my way. "Here we are," she said simply, her gaze guarded. There was a bite to the air, enough of a chill to flush her cheeks.

I couldn't have said I knew her particularly well, although we'd been as intimate as physically possible. But I had enough sense to know she was tense. I gathered she was trying to somehow snuff out this desire between us.

For once in my life, I might've been the more practical one in this equation. Well, perhaps not practical, rather realistic. This desire between us was a force of its own, too powerful to ignore, and I had every intention of feeding its fire.

I followed her up the steps and into her house, glancing around and taking in the open space. The muted evening light fell through the windows. When I saw her shiver, my eyes flicked to the woodstove in the corner. "Should you turn the heat up? I'll start a fire if you'd like," I offered.

She sighed, her eyes bouncing to me and then away. When she rubbed her palms on her arms again, a flash of protectiveness rose inside. Ignoring her, I strode to the far corner where the thermostat was mounted on the wall.

Before I had a chance to adjust it, she was at my side. With a huff, she swatted my hand away from it. "Oh for God's sake, don't be so high handed."

I turned, sliding my hands in my pockets to check the urge to pull her into my arms. Leaning my hips against the wall behind me, I eyed her, taking in the subtle shiver running through her, the flush on her cheeks and her gorgeous blue eyes.

"You're cold," I said, stating the obvious.

"So I am. It's not like I can't deal with it. I'd rather start a fire," she muttered, spinning away.

Once again, I took over, striding past her to the woodstove. "Got it."

I started to snag a piece of split wood in the small rack beside it when she grabbed it from me. "*I'll* get it," she snapped.

I stepped away, watching as she quickly stacked a few pieces of wood in the stove and stuffed kindling underneath. She knew how to build a fire, but then I'd have expected that. Inside of a few seconds, the blaze crackled.

Straightening, she glanced to me, crossing her arms over her chest. "Why are you being so bossy?"

"Offering to help build a fire when you're cold isn't bossy. I'd call it helpful."

Her eyes narrowed, and she snagged her bottom lip in her teeth. My eyes went right there, like a bee to honey. My cock swelled, and I didn't even try to stop it. I couldn't be near her and not want her, so I didn't even bother to try to tamp it down.

All of a sudden, her eyes glistened, and she spun away.

My reaction was visceral. I did *not* like seeing her upset. She walked to the windows facing out over the field with the fading sunset in the distance. Without thinking, I followed, watching as her shoulders rose and fell from behind with a swift, shaky breath. I slid my palms over her shoulders and down, carefully unfolding her tightly crossed arms and turning her into mine. I didn't know what the hell I was doing, but my need to comfort her rose above the flotsam in my mind.

She held her body tight, the tension radiating from her.

"Susannah. Look at me. Please."

After another shuddering breath, she looked up to me, her eyes bright with tears, her brow crinkling. I didn't know what it was about her, but she reached right inside of me, striking at places I didn't even know existed.

That little furrow between her brows was so damn endearing I wanted to kiss it. I had enough sense to know that wasn't wise, not right now.

"You can't just barge into my life like this, Ward." Her words were wobbly. A tear rolled down her cheek, and before I knew it, I was wiping it away with my thumb. "I'm as startled as you about this. I didn't expect to get pregnant. I mean, my God, we used condoms. I'm about to be a mother, and I'm pretty sure you weren't planning on being a father," she said flatly, another tear rolling down her cheeks. Another tear that I wiped away.

I stared at her, my heart tumbling oddly. I felt as if I was falling inside. I didn't know what the hell to do about any of this. I wanted her to just... Hell, I didn't know what I wanted. All we could do was face what we had to face. Since I lacked words, I let instinct drive me.

I pulled her against me, sliding one hand into her hair and the other around her hips to hold her close. Believe it or not, I wasn't trying to seduce her, not just then. I wanted her to feel better. She tensed at first and then relaxed against me, taking several shuddering breaths.

There was a soft tremor in her body. I wanted to smooth it away, to absorb it. Yet, this was all foreign to me. Sex was something I knew well. Comforting a woman, a woman who had a hold on me like no other and who was carrying our baby, well, it was safe to say I had less than zero experience with that.

After a few moments, the fine tremor disappeared, and she softened, shifting closer against me, her hips bumping into the ridge of my cock.

"Ignore it," I murmured, sifting my fingers through her silky curls.

Chapter Fifteen
SUSANNAH

The hard, hot length of Ward's cock pressed against my low belly. Despite his order to ignore it, I couldn't. Need unspooled inside, spiraling through me. A full body flush bloomed, my sex clenching. I could feel the slick heat of my desire, my panties wet just from the feel of him.

I was so rattled inside and out — from Ward, the effect he had on me, my pregnancy, and a jumble of overwhelming feelings. It unsettled me to savor his protectiveness and high handedness. I'd never have expected myself to want to sink into a man like that. I wanted nothing more than to let him sweep me into his embrace and make everything okay. When I was wrapped in his heat and warmth, that was how I felt— safe, protected, as if the rest of the world didn't exist and everything would somehow be okay.

In so many ways, it wasn't okay. I was flabbergasted by my pregnancy and by the certainty inside that I wanted to have this baby, even though it was sending my life careening down a path I hadn't even seen. It was shaking me to the core to realize Ward wasn't simply disappearing from my life.

His fingers sifted through my hair. His other palm slid up

and down my spine in warm passes, his touch strong and sure. Emotions were charging through me, a tangled mess inside. My doctor had warned me I would experience rapid hormonal shifts. I kept trying to chalk up my churned state to my pregnancy and hormones. Yet, a part of me knew, deep down inside, that the way Ward made me feel was feeding into all of this at a level I couldn't even comprehend.

I didn't want to ignore his cock. In fact, I wanted to lose myself in him and in the wild storm of need, desire, and emotion between us because that was the easy part. So when his palm slid down my spine again, cupping my bottom, I allowed myself to let go and arched into him. On the heels of another shuddering breath, my body wracked with need, I tumbled into the fire between us.

His hand stilled in my hair. "Susannah?"

I answered his question without a word, reaching between us and running my hand roughly over the length of his cock, almost groaning at the feel of him. I flicked my eyes up to his, catching his silver smoke gaze.

"You said it yourself, we do this quite well. No sense in pretending otherwise."

His eyes were locked to mine, heat flashing in them. Yet, he held still. "I think we need to talk first," he said, the mere sound of his gruff voice sending a hot shiver through me.

I stared at him, my pulse thudding so hard and fast I could hardly breathe. "I'd rather not," I murmured, sliding my palm up and down his cock, savoring the subtle growl that came from his throat. "Here's the thing, I'm having a baby. It's probably crazy, and we didn't plan on this, but it's happening. You said it yourself though. *I want you. You want me.* We're pretty good at this, so let's not worry about the rest right now."

Ward held my gaze, his eyes flickering with something I didn't know how to interpret. That was the funny thing with us. I knew him intimately in the physical sense. Frankly, sex with him was so damn good and so intimate, I had no idea what to make of it. Yet, beyond that, we didn't know each other particularly well. There was still the inconvenient, awkward issue that we were working together now.

"And we have to figure out how we're going to deal with this with the crew. It might be best if I switch to a different crew," I managed over the thundering beat of my heart.

Ward shook his head, his eyes narrowing. "No."

I should've been annoyed with his tendency to assume he could call the shots, but I could've cared less. That was the thing about tumbling into the fire with him. I could forget everything else. I started unbuttoning his jeans. Lightning fast, he reached between us, catching both of my hands in one of his.

When I tried to tug free, he didn't give. "Let me go," I muttered.

"Only if you promise to stop avoiding me. I'm all for this..." He paused, palming my ass with his free hand and rocking his arousal into me as if to punctuate his point. "But don't run hot and cold on me."

Staring into his gaze, a wave of emotion rocked me. I'd known it four years ago when I let myself have a taste of him. Whatever lay between us was unlike anything I'd ever felt before. My need for him had such a wild, reckless edge to it, so strong it had frightened me. Yet, that had been one night. I'd walked away believing I'd never see him again.

Now he stood before me, every glorious, crazy sexy inch of him—mine for the taking. And I was pregnant and my emotions ran the gamut. His request was fair. I didn't usually run hot and cold on anyone. But then, no man had ever affected me with such power that I wanted to shy away. His gaze was implacable. I knew he wouldn't budge, so I swallowed, trying to tamp down the emotion threatening to overwhelm me.

"I won't. I'm just..."

All of a sudden, tears pricked at my eyes again and my throat felt tight. This was precisely why I preferred to lose myself in sensation. It was so much easier than thinking. "It's just a lot, and I'm trying to figure it out," I said, my words thick.

I felt so vulnerable with him, and it made me want to run away again. But there was nowhere to run, nowhere to hide —from his far too perceptive gaze, from the strength of his embrace. He surprised me again, his hand easing loose around mine. And then his lips were feathering across my cheek, dusting along my ear and down my neck—his touch gentle and so hot, I could barely withstand it, almost melting into a puddle at his feet.

I fumbled with the buttons on his jeans, nearly frantic for him now, moaning when I felt the velvety skin of his cock. Right there, no barrier to keep me from wrapping my palm around it. I'd never once in my life contemplated whether I cared if a man wore boxers or briefs. I loved the fact Ward wore neither. His breath hissed between his teeth and then his mouth was on mine, his tongue sweeping inside —commanding, demanding, and taking over our kiss immediately.

His hand, which had been sifting gently through my hair, tightened its grip, tangling roughly. The sharp sting of the tug on my scalp sent sparks flying through me, a pleasure pain so intense I moaned into his mouth. Our tongues dueled in the deep, wet, openmouthed kiss—so wild and so hot, my knees nearly buckled. It was rather convenient to have his strength holding me up, his palm squeezing my ass. He lifted me against him, and I curled my legs around his hips.

He held me with ease. I loved it, loved that feeling of being encompassed by his strength. I reluctantly released his cock, wrapping my arms around his broad shoulders and tearing my lips free to gulp in some air.

Ward didn't miss a beat, his lips blazing a trail along my jawline, his tongue teasing the shell of my ear, the heat of his breath sending a hot shiver through my entire body. He nipped my neck before lifting his head as he turned to carry me toward the stairs.

"Bedroom," he growled, his words more of an order than a question.

I nudged my chin toward the stairs. "Upstairs to the right."

He walked with me, his stride strong and sure, like everything about him. The feel of his hard cock rubbing against me through the layers of fabric between us, a subtle abrasion over my clit, sent sharp streaks of pleasure through me. He made me crazy. It was everything—his power, the feel of his arms holding me tight, and the hard length of him nestled between my thighs.

I nipped at his neck, running a hand through his hair. I loved the taste of him, salty with a woodsy, musky scent. His foot caught the top stair, and he stumbled slightly, steadying us quickly, never once losing his firm grip on me.

"Fuck, Susannah," he murmured. "Killin' me."

I lifted my head, a sly grin curling my lips. With the clear knowledge of how out of control he made me, I loved knowing maybe, just maybe, he was as close to the edge as I was.

"Hurry up," I said, my voice husky.

His palm gripped my ass, and he squeezed, his fingers grazing so close to that sweet spot between my thighs, my hips rocked against him. He never broke his gait, dipping his head to nip at my neck. Everywhere he touched me was like a bolt of lightning.

"Here?"

I'd been so wrapped up in the taste of his skin along his collarbone, I'd forgotten where we were. Lifting my head, I found the door to my bedroom straight ahead. "Oh, you're good at following instructions," I said with a giggle, nodding and tapping my toe against the door.

He freed one hand, reaching behind us to turn the knob and kick the door open. Spinning around, he walked straight to my bed in the center of the room, pausing with me still held firmly in his embrace. His eyes caught mine, dark and intent. For a loaded moment, we stared at each other, the air heavy around us. With a growl, he claimed my mouth again—a hot, wet, breath-stealing kiss that melted me inside and out. I was nearly limp in his arms by the time he drew away after one last deep stroke of his tongue.

Cupping my bottom, he rocked his erection into me, sending a spike of pleasure straight through the center of my body. He eyed me for a beat as I tugged at his T-shirt.

"Off," I huffed.

His mouth curled into a smile. "Kinda hard to get it off with you in the way."

He stared at me, his gaze considering, and then slowly eased me down. I started to yank at his clothes, but he stepped back and had me naked in no time. No surprise, but he was efficient. My clothes lay in a rumpled array on the floor in a matter of seconds. He lifted me, stretching me out on the bed, his knee coming to rest between my thighs.

Naked, my breasts feeling achy, and my nipples puckered, I was flushed inside and out and soaking wet. Just looking up at him made my sex clench. I could feel the moisture between my thighs. I wasn't even thinking when I reached between them, desperate for relief, dragging my fingers through my folds.

His eyes darkened. "No," he said, his tone brooking no dissent.

I couldn't believe it, but I stopped, taking my hand away and letting it fall to the bed. Bending a knee, I rolled one thigh open, never once looking away from his searing gaze. "If you won't let me take care of it, you'd better."

His eyes raked down my body, pausing at the apex of my thighs. My sex felt swollen with need, clenching simply at the feel of his gaze on me. I allowed my eyes to soak him in. He stood above me, his jeans half open, his cock hard, thick and erect. My channel clenched again. His eyes snagged mine, the need there so raw it took my breath away.

I swiped my tongue across my lips. "You have too many clothes on."

Ward didn't say a word, but his gaze darkened further. He reached behind his neck, lifting his shirt off in one motion and baring his hard muscled chest for me. I started to rise on my elbows, but he shook his head sharply. The mattress rose as he pushed away, kicking his boots off and shoving his jeans down. Leaning over me, he trailed his fingers from my breastbone down the center of my body, my belly fluttering under his touch.

"I love your red curls here," he murmured as his fingers slipped through them, one finger sliding through my folds.

A whimper escaped as my hips arched up into him. "So tell me Zanna..." My eyes flashed up to his. My hips flexed again with another pass of his finger, the blunt, calloused tip coasting over my clit and sending sparks of pleasure everywhere. "What do you want?"

The sound of his voice alone felt like a caress. I wanted him—every hard, thick inch of him buried inside of me. So I said so. "You. Inside of me."

He nodded slowly. "We'll get there, but I need something first."

Then, his hands pushed my thighs apart, and his lips trailed kisses along the insides of my calves. By the time his mouth reached the apex of my thighs, my hips were writhing, and I was panting.

There was foreplay and then there was what Ward did—torture and pleasure tangled together. He sank a finger in my channel. I felt the burn of his gaze on me, and I managed to drag my eyes open.

"I'm going to taste you now."

His words were so blunt and direct, my pussy clenched at the mere thought of what he was about to do. Then, his mouth was on the core of me, his fingers teasing along with his lips and tongue.

"You taste so fucking good."

Ward took no prisoners. With a maddening mix of rough and gentle, his hands and his mouth devoured me. Pleasure spun tighter and tighter inside. Caught in a current of sensation so intense, I lost sight of everything but the feel of his mouth against me, his tongue and fingers making me crazy. He drew back for a moment.

"Zanna."

No man had ever used that nickname with me, and certainly no one had ever used it the way he did. His voice made love to the nickname. It felt like a brand on me, as if he were claiming me.

"Look at me. I want to watch your face when you come."

I couldn't have denied him even if I wanted to. I didn't. My eyelids heavy, I dragged them open. The moment my eyes met his, I was locked into his gaze. He dipped his head again, his eyes dropping down as he dragged his tongue across my folds and buried his fingers in me. With a swirl of his tongue around my clit, he caught it lightly in his teeth.

I flew apart as he lifted his head, his gaze snagging mine again. Pleasure unraveled inside, fracturing me and rocking my body with wave after wave. Caught in the undertow, I cried out. The only word I seemed capable of speaking was his name—again and again and again.

Boneless, I felt his fingers draw away, and then the feel of his lips and the rough scrape of his stubble on my belly. He mapped his way up my body, lingering at my breasts, teasing my nipples with his tongue, a score of his teeth and a pinch of his fingers.

It was no matter I'd just had an earth shattering climax. By the time his weight settled over me and I felt his cock resting against my folds, hard and pulsing, I was already frantic with need again. My hands mapped his muscled chest and back, gripping his hard ass. I dragged my tongue along his neck, the subtle taste of him something I needed like air—at least in this moment, spinning in the eddies of desire from my explosive climax.

"Zanna."

Opening my eyes, I found his waiting, flashing silver and seeing right through me. I was tangled up in pure, raw sensuality and need mingling with an intimacy I could hardly bear.

He rocked his hips against me, his cock sliding across my clit. Between my own desire and the madness he'd wrought with his mouth, I was slippery wet. His elbows rested at my shoulders, one of his hands brushing a few tangled curls off of my forehead. When he rocked his hips into me again, a whimper escaped. I felt so desperate when I was with him, as if nothing could slake my need. Only him.

His hands slid down my shoulders, catching mine in his and stretching them up above my head. My body arched and flexed, my breasts pressing into his hard chest. My nipples were so tight they ached.

With another rock of his hips, his cock slid across my clit again, sending a shock of pleasure spiraling through me. "I need you," I gasped.

"Right here," he murmured, his voice soft and steely at once.

"No, I need you inside me," I demanded, curling my legs around him and arching against him. "Don't make me wait."

Though he had all the control, without a doubt, he didn't make me wait. With my hands held tight in his, he adjusted the angle of his hips and started to ease into me. When I felt his hard, thick length begin to stretch me, I got restless, rocking into him, needing the rough feeling of him filling me.

"Ward," I gasped, his name a breathy plea.

For a moment, I thought he was going to tease, but his hands curled tightly to mine, he drew back and sank home in one swift surge.

Chapter Sixteen
WARD

Susannah's channel pulsed around me, tight, wet, and hot. I was clinging by my fingernails to the edge of my control. Tasting her made me crazy. Everything about her called to the most primal parts of me. I held still, adjusting to the feel of her creamy clench throbbing around me.

It was a damn good thing I'd never had unprotected sex before. If I had, I probably never would've been as religious as I'd been about using condoms. Because, sweet hell, being inside of Susannah with nothing between us was sheer heaven.

She flexed into me, her taut nipples pressing against me, damp from my attentions. I managed to open my eyes to find her gaze hazy and unfocused. Her lips were swollen and puffy from our kisses, her skin flushed with a sheen of desire, and her strawberry curls a tangled mess on the pillows.

My heart gave a hard thump, a wave of emotion hitting me. The depth of this connection with her was so unfamiliar, I had no idea how to interpret it. All I knew was what I wanted — to be buried deep inside of her as close as physically possible and to feel her fly apart in my arms while I found my own release. I loved having her stretched out underneath me.

She didn't hesitate to relinquish control. Knowing how strong and powerful she was, how fearless she was by nature, there was something even more intense about her giving in to me. My body moved on its own accord, drawing back and sinking inside of her—again and again and again. I heard myself saying her name almost reverently, my voice slurred, drunk with desire for her.

My release was so close, but I wanted her to fly apart before I did. So with my balls tightening, pleasure lashing at me, and my hips sinking into her, I reached between us, pressing my thumb over her clit. When she cried out, her body flexed under me and her pussy clamped down around my cock.

My release hit me hard, a wave of pleasure pulling me under. The power of it was so intense, I didn't even hear myself calling out her name, my hands gripping hers tightly and every muscle in my body going taut as I powered into her one last time. Collapsing against her, reverberating with the force of my climax, I rolled onto my back, bringing her atop me.

Her weight felt good on me. She was soft and relaxed, her breath gusting against my shoulder. After a few moments, she lifted her head and rested her chin on her hand. Feeling her eyes on me, I opened mine.

"Well," she said, a slight smile hitching the corner of her mouth.

"Well what?"

"Did you want to talk now?"

I couldn't say why, but I laughed.

"What's so funny?"

Sifting my fingers through her hair, I savored the feel of her against me. "I can barely think. I'm starting to think we'll never get around to talking. I can't seem to be near you and not want you."

At my words, her cheeks flushed and her channel clenched around me. My cock twitched in response, and I slid my palm down her back to cup her ass. Because, let me tell you, she had a sweet ass.

"Yeah, we seem to have a problem with that," she replied, the pink on her cheeks deepening.

"How is it a problem? You said it yourself, we're pretty good at it."

She giggled, and I loved it. My heart squeezed, emotion rocking me. Still uncertain how to handle my feelings, I did the only thing that made sense when I was with her, I touched her...more. Angling my head, I dusted kisses on her neck. She tasted so damn good.

I was prepared for her to insist we talk. Hell, tonight I'd been trying to insist. But she didn't. Her skin flushed and heat banked in her gaze. Before I knew it, my cock was hardening inside of her and she rose up, rocking against me. All I knew was the feel of her around me—the slick, clenching heat of her channel, her skin like silk, her nipples dusky pink and puckered tight. My release poured into her as she came with a rough cry, arching back and calling out my name.

We fell asleep, her curled on top of me with me still buried deep inside of her.

Chapter Seventeen
WARD

The following day, I woke up with Susannah still curled up against me. At some point during the night, I'd slipped out of her. Yet, I could feel the damp heat of her pussy against my hip and my cock growing hard the moment I became conscious. So I took her again and then had to resist the urge to take her again in the shower. It was safe to say I couldn't get enough of her.

She made coffee for me and offered to make breakfast, teasing that she needed to make do with tea for now. We were downright domestic. Yet, when I made a vague attempt to talk as she'd originally insisted we needed to do, she dismissed the idea.

If this were any other woman or any other situation, I wouldn't get frustrated. Yet, everything with Susannah felt loaded. All of it tangled up in the reality that, in the foreseeable future, she would have our baby. The concept of *domestic* would take on a profound meaning.

I managed to keep a lid on it. If only because I sensed if I pushed, she'd bolt.

When I left to go to the station, she told me she'd see me

there later. That was the only moment where I saw shadows pass through her eyes. Even if I didn't want to face it, I knew she was right. We had to figure out the work situation.

My thoughts took a sharp turn here. Susannah was pregnant, and she was a hotshot firefighter. Sometimes I could be king of the obvious. Yet, I hadn't considered these two facts together. My heart gave a funny little tumble in my chest, surprising me with the weight of emotion rocking me.

Shoving those thoughts away, I went to work.

Later that afternoon, Cade and Beck came to meet with me for the planned meeting with Chad. The meeting went about as well as you would expect. In short, it was shitty.

"Fuck you," was Chad's response.

I didn't need Beck and Cade to take the heat for me, but I was damn glad they were there. They had the background that I didn't with Chad and with the crew.

I held Chad's flat brown gaze. "You're entitled to your opinion, but the decision's final." I didn't care to enlighten him further, seeing as he'd argued every point thus far.

Chad flicked his gaze from me to Cade and then Beck, his lips curling in a sneer. When his eyes made their way back to me, he shook his head. "They know you got a thing for Susannah?"

I kept my expression level, but I was fucking pissed. "Not sure what your point is," I countered.

"Whether he has a thing for Susannah, or anyone here, frankly has nothing to do with this," Beck said flatly. "We just outlined the reasons for our decision. Taking it out on Ward isn't going to help your case. If Ward wasn't here, we'd still be firing you."

Cade nodded affirmatively. If he had any reaction to Chad's comment, it didn't show on his face.

To my relief, Chad didn't choose to drag it out further. He stood, kicking his chair back. "Fuck you guys anyway. Be good to get the hell out of here." He slammed out of my office.

I stood, quickly striding after him. "You'll need to get your stuff and leave."

Chad muttered something over his shoulder, but he didn't fight me on it. He went straight to his locker, got his gear and left.

The timing was good, if only by chance. None of the crew happened to be in the back area when he stormed his way out. Walking back to my office, I found Beck returning from the hallway with three cups of coffee balanced carefully in his hands.

"Here ya go," he said, sliding all three cups onto the round table in the corner of my office. I sank into one of the chairs at the table with a sigh and grabbed a cup, taking a long swallow.

"Thanks," I said, tilting my cup in his direction.

Beck nodded. "No problem. Coffee's always good after a shitty meeting."

"That it is," I replied, my focus elsewhere. I was contemplating whether I needed to bother addressing Chad's comment about Susannah. The thing was, I didn't give a damn what anybody thought. Not about me. But I knew Susannah would care. Whether I wanted to care or not, there were some team dynamics to address.

I trusted Beck and Cade, despite only knowing them a short time. I figured I might as well cut to the chase. "Thanks for sitting in on that with me. I don't mind him being pissed at me, but it was good to have the back up from you guys since you have more history with him."

Cade nodded, taking a sip from his coffee, his gaze considering. But he didn't say a word.

Beck, the more chatty of the two, shrugged. "He

behaved exactly as I expected. His attitude is why he should've been fired a hell of a lot sooner."

Glancing between them, I took a sip of coffee and set it down. "Mind if I ask you guys for some advice?"

True to form, Cade simply shook his head. Beck, on the other hand, flashed a grin. "Oh, we love giving advice. Throw it our way."

"That comment he made about Susannah? It's true. We trained together years ago. I never thought I'd see her again. Hell, when I took this position, I didn't know she was here until after I accepted it. I'm trusting you guys not to say a damn word to anyone about this. She'll have my head and probably more than that if she finds out I spoke to you guys about it. To make matters more complicated, she's pregnant."

Beck almost spit his coffee out. Cade was snapped out of his generally calm demeanor, his eyes widening and his mouth falling open slightly.

"Damn," Cade said. "Not what I expected you to say. Is the baby yours?"

"Definitely."

Beck scrubbed his hands through his hair, for once not teasing. "Holy shit. What the hell is she going to do?"

"She wants to have the baby." The moment I said that, my heart tightened, emotion thickening my throat. I tried to shake it free because, while I trusted them, I wasn't ready to get all emotional with them. Definitely not my thing.

Cade had collected himself and tilted his head to the side. "Well, there's the obvious issue that you two are about to have a baby. That's kind of a big deal. On a practical note, there's crew stuff to deal with. But it might be simpler than you think."

"What do you mean?" Beck interjected, conveniently asking my question for me.

Cade shrugged. "Well, Susannah can only work for so long in this type of job when she's pregnant. Haven't checked the protocol in a while, but I think after she's past the first trimester, she's not even supposed to go out in the field. That might solve your problem for you. When she returns, might be better if she's on a different crew."

I shook my head sharply. "No." I didn't care to contemplate Susannah being apart from me for weeks at a time. Simultaneously, I didn't care to consider what that said about me and how I felt about her.

Beck arched a brow. "You think you're going to tell Susannah what to do? Don't think that'll go over well."

I chuckled. "You think she'll fight me on it?"

"You mean staying on your crew?" he asked

At my nod, Cade spoke up. "I've known Susannah for years. She does *not* like being told what to do."

The reality of this conversation hit me like a brick. I was carrying on as if it was a done deal Susannah and I would be together. I was screwed. It was like a train plowing into my life on a track I hadn't even known existed. I had no fucking idea what I was doing.

Something must've shown on my face because Beck glanced between Cade and me, a sly smile tugging at the corners of his mouth. "You're looking like you had no idea she might mean that much to you. Take it from me, just go with it. Susannah is awesome, and you look... What's the word?"

"Whipped," Cade offered helpfully.

Chapter Eighteen
SUSANNAH

Hands on my hips, I stood outside, watching as one of our crewmembers came dashing out of the burning house. The wind was gusting high, but clouds were rolling in. We'd been called to a fire in a neighboring town. A fishing lodge had caught fire when a chimney stovepipe got too hot. The lodge was sprawling and had guests, which meant we had our hands full. At the moment, the crew was focused on ensuring all the guests were out safely.

Meanwhile, I was annoyed, frankly annoyed didn't quite capture how I felt. I was pissed. Ward, being high-handed as hell, had kept me on duty by the truck. He'd actually *ordered* me not to enter the building. I didn't like feeling useless. One of the things I loved about being a firefighter was charging in and helping. I'd never been one who preferred to hang back on the outskirts. Yet, that was where I was.

A few of us needed to stay by the trucks. Ward, of course, was in the thick of it. He'd entered and left the building several times, escorting a number of guests out safely, along with the rest of our crew.

Mingling with my irritation towards him was the fact I

was concerned about him. This wasn't a foreign feeling, generally speaking. Hell, when you were on a crew like this, you bonded with all of your crewmembers. With the exception of Chad, who I was relieved to see Ward had dispatched quickly, I was close to my entire team. I'd been on this crew for three years now.

Being concerned for my crewmembers was a common feeling. Yet, the worry I felt for Ward was totally different. Just now, my heart was pounding and my chest felt tight because I watched him run back into the building. Meanwhile, I was stuck on the sidelines.

Hours later, we were back at the station, tired, gritty and grimy. The guys were crowding the shower room that they shared, while I headed into the smaller shower room for female firefighters. There weren't many of us at the moment, a whopping total of two, myself and Harlow May. Harlow had joined Cade's crew about a month ago. She was tall and strong, and easily held her own. She was also gorgeous with her glossy dark hair and dark brown eyes, yet she appeared oblivious to this and was so tomboyish she fit in easily with the guys.

I was rinsing the soap out of my hair when I heard Harlow's voice. "God, sometimes I'm so glad you're here. I'd hate being the only woman in this whole station," she said by way of greeting.

She turned the water on as I lifted my head and glanced over with a smile. "Oh, I get the feeling. For the three years I've been here, you're only the second woman who's been through here."

We showered in silence for a few more minutes. As I was turning the water off and walking past her, she followed suit. We were in the small locker room when she glanced my way, her eyes a tad curious.

"Everything okay?" I asked.

Harlow stared at me for a beat as if considering her

words. Finally, she spoke. "Not to be nosy, but are you pregnant?"

My mouth actually fell open, and I felt my cheeks heat. Fuck. The look on my face must've given the answer away because she smiled softly. "So you are then?"

I nodded slowly. "How can you tell? I'm not that far along." Almost seven weeks to be specific, but I didn't say that aloud.

She lifted her shoulder in a shrug. "I was pregnant before." She held her hands up to her breasts and then patted her tummy. "It's not much, but I can tell. Not that I've been staring at you, but, well, you've changed a little bit."

The wheels spun in my mind. I knew she didn't have a child, so I wasn't sure what that meant. As if reading my expression, she explained. "I had a miscarriage four months in," she said matter-of-factly.

"I'm sorry," I offered, uncertain what else to say.

Sadness flashed in the depths of her eyes. "It's life, I suppose. The timing was terrible, and I can't say I had planned to get pregnant. But once I was, I wanted to have the baby. I had an accident out in the field, a bad fall. The doctor said that may or may not have caused my miscarriage, but still. It's none of my business, but if you really want your baby, just think about what you do out in the field. You should probably tell Ward what's going on, so he can make the call on whether you should be on light duty."

I stared at her, hard, my thoughts tumbling every which way. Fear stabbed at me—the very idea I could have a miscarriage making me want to cry. Intellectually, I knew it was a possibility in every pregnancy, but nothing was intellectual now. Everything was very real. I gave myself a mental shake, forcing my attention back to her. "I'm so sorry that happened to you."

Harlow shrugged, although her gaze was somber. "It's okay. It was two years ago now. As I said, it wasn't the best timing. Plus the guy who I was with, who would've been the father... Well, it's safe to say he was an asshole. Or more accurately, a hound dog. He got around. I promised myself if something like that happened again, I wouldn't be dating an asshole." She paused, her gaze careful. "I'm guessing you plan to keep the baby."

At my nod, she smiled softly. "Congratulations."

We stood there, staring at each other. I had no idea what else to say at this point. I was so freaked out by her experience, I was scrambling to get a grip inside. I was saved by the station intercom going off, and Maisie reporting another call to a fire on the outskirts of town.

Though all three crews stationed here were hotshot crews trained to be sent out into the backcountry, we also responded to local calls. Although Willow Brook wasn't by any means a large town, we served every community in the surrounding area until we bumped into Anchorage. As such, we were busy as hell.

Harlow hurried back into her gear, racing out to touch base with Cade. Meanwhile, I didn't know what to do. As irritated as I'd been at Ward's call earlier, learning that Harlow had a miscarriage scared me near to death.

I hadn't been fully dressed when the intercom call went out, and I stood there contemplating what to do. Technically, I should go check in with Ward, but I figured he was busy. As if conjured by thought alone, there was a knock on the locker room door.

"Susannah?"

The sound of Ward's voice saying my name set my pulse off and emotion rocking through me. "You dressed?" he asked through the door.

"Give me a sec," I called, quickly tugging my jeans on and throwing a T-shirt on.

Stepping to the door, I opened it. Ward stood there, already in a fresh set of gear. Gesturing him in, I closed the door behind us. His gaze swept over me, the heat of it searing me. He stayed by the doorway, exuding a sense of control, as if he was trying to keep something in check. His eyes locked to mine, he said, "Harlow mentioned you might want to check in with me about going back out."

I nodded, conflicted inside. Part of me was still angry with him. I didn't like him making the decision on limits for me. Yet, I loved how protected he made me feel. Much as I loved that, I also abhorred the sense of weakness it represented for me.

Before I thought about it, I was blurting out what Harlow told me. "She had a miscarriage, an accident in the field. I don't know..." My words trailed off as emotion thickened my throat.

Ward flipped the bolt on the door behind him and closed the distance between us, stopping immediately in front of me, so close I could feel the heat of him.

"I know you were pissed earlier, but that's why I asked you to stay back. We need to talk about this, to have a plan. If you're going to fight me on it, I don't know what to do."

"What am I to you?" I asked, the question slipping out unbidden.

His eyes flashed silver and smoke as he stared at me. "All I know is I don't want to put you or our baby at risk."

My heart hammered in my chest, and that need—a need very specific to Ward—rose within. It felt as if Ward was pounding at the doors guarding my heart. I couldn't seem to separate out my desire from my emotions. At least not when it came to him.

"For tonight, I'll stay back if that's okay." I hadn't planned to say that, but it was what came out.

His expression softened, relief washing over his features as the tension eased. He pulled me swiftly into his arms, into his strong encompassing embrace. Suddenly, I wanted to cry. But now definitely wasn't the time for that. He needed to leave. I swallowed through the thickness in my throat and stepped away. "You have to go, what will you tell the crew?"

"That you don't feel good. That's it." He opened his mouth as if to say something else and then snapped it shut. "I should go."

At that, he spun away, and I watched him walk through the door, my eyes tracking the swing of his shoulders.

The moment he was out of sight, my mind swung into battle with itself. I couldn't quite believe I'd given into my fear so easily. That wasn't who I was. Yet, Harlow's experience was hard to ignore.

Chapter Nineteen
WARD

Returning to the station late that night, I showered and dressed before sinking into the chair in my office and wondering what the hell to do. Today had been nothing unusual for the crew. In fact, it had been a light day for us. Being able to deal with a fire and return to the station in the same day was safer and easier than being flown out in the middle of nowhere and fighting fires largely on our own.

I'd known Susannah was furious with me earlier today. My call to keep her by the truck was an instant decision, one I hadn't discussed with her in advance. Frankly, a decision I hadn't considered myself before. All I'd known was I couldn't bear to put her in danger, so I'd simply done what I had to do to keep her out of it.

When Harlow came and told me to check on Susannah, I'd freaked out inside, worried something had happened while she was in the shower. That was how ridiculous this was. I didn't doubt her strength for a second. Yet, the need to protect her and our baby rose above everything else.

When she told me about Harlow's miscarriage, and I'd seen the fear in her eyes, I'd been so fucking relieved she made the call on her own to stay back tonight. Now, I was staring down the reality of what we faced.

Her question kept ringing in my mind, mocking me. "What am I to you?" she'd asked.

Two words came to mind.

Everything. Mine.

There I was sitting in my office in the late evening while my crew went off to the bar. All I wanted was to go find her and curl up with her. Because if she was in my arms, then I knew she was safe.

I tugged my phone out of my pocket. Not letting myself think about it much further, I pulled up her number and sent a text.

On my way.

Chapter Twenty
SUSANNAH

On my way.

The moment I saw his text, I was at war with myself, my emotions battling with each other. He was so high handed, so alpha. He annoyed the hell out of me, and I loved it.

My fingers itched to tap out a reply. Yet, I knew it would be childish. The truth was, I wanted him here. Restless, I decided to clean the kitchen. Not that there was much to clean, but I had a few dishes, and I needed to organize the refrigerator. I had my head inside said refrigerator when I heard a knock on the door as it opened and then Ward's voice.

Before I could even back out of the refrigerator, I felt him come up behind me and his hands slide over the curve of my hips and bottom. Straightening, I spun around, closing the refrigerator door behind me. The cool air had chilled me, and my nipples were tight little points. I felt his gaze flick down and then back up. My cheeks heated.

"That's not because of you," I said, almost annoyed at my body's response. It hadn't been true initially, yet the moment I looked at him, every cell of my body hummed.

When he grinned, that dangerous grin of his, my belly obediently executed a flip. Further annoyed with myself, I skipped topics. "How did everything go?"

He arched a brow, as if uncertain what I meant, I clarified. "The fire."

"Nothing major. Some guy decided to have a giant brushfire and ended up catching the forest beside his house on fire while he was at it. One thing I've noticed here is burn restrictions are rather lax."

I chuckled. "Oh yeah. Most towns have blanket fire bans when it's really dry, but most areas also allow permits for the whole summer. Makes for some problems."

His gaze sobered as he stared at me, his hands still resting on my hips where they'd remained when I turned. "We need to talk."

I'd done a lot of thinking this afternoon and come to a few of my own conclusions. The one thing I wasn't quite ready to sort out was what to do about us per se. But as for the rest, I considered myself somewhat sensible.

"I know. I've thought about it since this afternoon. I'll talk to my doctor tomorrow. She already said she could give me a letter clearing me from heavy work. The rest of the crew doesn't have to know anything other than I'm pregnant. At least not right now. I figure that buys me some time," I explained.

His eyes held mine, the intensity of his gaze sending a rush of emotion through me. He was quiet, only nodding after a beat.

"Are you going to say anything?" I finally asked.

"I think that's a good idea," he finally said.

Before I could say anything else, his lips were on mine, his hand tangling in my hair, and I was swept away into the crazy, intense heartbeat of intimacy that pounded between us.

Which was perfectly fine. The less we talked, the better.

Chapter Twenty-One
SUSANNAH

Dr. Jenkins leaned back in her chair, adjusting her glasses. After a moment, she spoke. "I'm happy to write you the letter, and frankly, I'm relieved you have enough sense to do this. I'm the first to tell you I encourage my patients not to worry about their pregnancies. I tell them the truth—that women have been having babies since the beginning of time. It's a normal, common part of life. Yet, I don't have many patients whose job is as grueling as yours."

I sat on the examination table before her, chilly in the thin cotton gown I wore, twisting my hands in my lap and nodding along with her words. Before I knew it, a tear was rolling down my cheek. Dr. Jenkins stood and leaned against the table beside me, snagging a box of tissues off the counter and handing me one.

"It's none of my business, and if you don't want to talk about it, that's fine. But I'm wondering who the father is, and if he's involved. Like I told you, you're going to experience some emotional swings due to the hormonal changes. Yet, you haven't said a word about who the father is and how that's affecting you. By no means is this a lecture. Some of the best mothers I know are single mothers. Yet if the father is involved, it would be good for him to perhaps be a part of a few of our appointments," she said gently.

I was coming to realize my doctor knew me better than I'd thought. How she could so easily see into what lay behind my tears was beyond me. I blew my nose and nodded.

My mind flashed back to the night before when Ward took me on the kitchen counter, powering into me so hard and fast, I saw stars, nearly limp from the force of my climax. The intimacy I felt with him was startling. Yet, we didn't talk about it, and I sure as hell didn't want to. When Dr. Jenkins said my hormones would affect me, I wondered if she meant I'd become sex crazed.

Although, I knew the news of my pregnancy was a surprise to Ward, I had no idea if he'd want to come to these appointments. I wasn't so sure I wanted him to. I was starting to worry about myself. Because I was having flashes of hopes and wishes and dreams that I'd never considered—all of them with Ward in the starring role.

I felt like a foolish girl, wanting the wedding and the picket fence and our baby. Something I'd never known I wanted that much. Yet without Ward being the man in all of those equations, I didn't want any of these things. I certainly didn't think they made much sense as it was. I chalked it up to the overwhelming circumstances.

I tugged another tissue out of the box and glanced over to Dr. Jenkins. Her gaze was warm and kind behind her glasses. She smiled softly. "Well, this might not make you feel better, but it's the truth. Whether pregnancies are planned or whether people are married or not, in my experience, none of those things have anything to do with how things go in the long run."

I took a shuddering breath and nodded. "I'll talk to him. It might be good for him to come to one of these appointments." Even though that was what I said, my feelings about including him were muddled. I wasn't so sure it was a good idea.

She stepped away, clicking on the laptop screen and looking at her calendar. "We can schedule your first ultrasound in a few weeks, and then the next one between eighteen and twenty-two weeks. At that appointment, you'll be able to find out if it's a boy or a girl. If you want to know, that is," she said matter-of-factly. "Let's get these on the calendar now. I'll have our receptionist give you the schedule on your way out." She tapped a few keys as she spoke.

Tears rolled down my cheeks anew, this time not from sadness, but from a rushing sense of joy. I might not have planned this baby, I might not be prepared, and I might be a hot mess inside about what it meant for Ward and me, but there was a tangled joy rising through the scrum.

Late that evening, my phone buzzed on the kitchen counter. Anticipation rose swiftly inside. Ward and I hadn't spoken yet today. I'd called out of work altogether because I simply wasn't up for it. When I spun the phone on the counter and saw a text from him, I grinned, a giddy sense of joy bubbling up.

On my way.

Glancing at the clock, I calculated he would be here in about fifteen minutes. Restless, I started folding the laundry. It gave me something to do while I waited. When I heard his truck rolling down the driveway, I had to hold back the urge to go meet him on the deck.

When he walked inside, I looked up from the couch as I put a pair of socks in the laundry basket. Closing the door behind him, he paused, his eyes locking to mine from across the room. It felt as if a band of electricity flickered to life between us, the air alive and heavy. He toed his boots off and shrugged out of his jacket, hanging it on the coat rack by the door.

"Have you had dinner?" he asked.

At the shake of my head, he smiled slowly. "Good, I just called in a pizza. I didn't want to impose, but I'm fucking starving," he said bluntly.

I stared at him, thoughts tumbling through my mind. My words surprised me. "My doctor wants to know if you want to come to any of the appointments," I blurted out.

The moment I spoke, I wanted to take the words back. *Hormones, hormones.* I didn't need to turn this into more than it was.

Ward had started to walk across the room and came to a stop dead in the center of it, his eyes widening in shock. "I guess I hadn't even thought about that."

Anxious that I'd even said anything, I shrugged, trying to play it off. "It's no big deal. I wouldn't have mentioned it if she hadn't."

I was relieved to hear the sound of a car coming down the driveway already. Our awkward conversation was conveniently interrupted by the pizza delivery driver.

Chapter Twenty-Two
WARD

The sun angling through the windows woke me the following morning. As my consciousness filtered in, I felt relaxed and downright amazing. Oh, and I was rock hard and ready. With Susannah's warm, soft body curled up against mine, I supposed that was all but a given.

Last night, we had pizza and then lounged on the couch. I discovered she didn't care much for television, but could easily get sucked into sci-fi in a hot minute. Just thinking about that, a smile tugged at the corners of my mouth.

My hands had a mind of their own. I'd conveniently woken with one of her breasts cupped in my palm. Savoring its lush weight, I brushed my thumb across her nipple, gratified when it puckered tight under my touch. I let my fingers drift across to tease her other nipple, my cock hardening further with every moment I allowed myself to explore her body.

Though she'd relaxed somewhat when we were watching television, I'd sensed she was guarded last night. In fact, I didn't know if I would've been sleeping with her here in my arms if it hadn't been for the fact that she'd fallen asleep on the couch. I'd glanced down to see her sound asleep, her feet tucked up under her hips and her head resting against my shoulder.

Without thinking about it, I'd lifted her up and carried her to bed. After stripping her down to her T-shirt and underwear, I'd climbed in bed with her, promising myself I wasn't staying to have sex. My intentions had been pure last night, but this morning was something else. She was too close and her body was too tempting with her musky scent drifting around me.

With her lush bottom pressed into my cock, it didn't matter that there were two layers of fabric between us. As I teased her nipples, she shifted in her sleep, a soft moan escaping her lips. I couldn't resist. I had to taste her. With my free hand, I brushed her hair away from her cheek and dipped my head, dusting kisses along the soft skin of her neck.

Her legs shifted, and she started to roll towards me. I wasn't sure I wanted her to wake up because I was worried she'd start thinking. Shoving that worry away, I focused on sensation. She tasted so good, sweet and salty. I lightly pinched one of her nipples between my thumb and forefinger, almost growling in satisfaction when she arched into my palm.

"Ward," she murmured, her voice husky from sleep.

"Mmm, hmm?"

Another moan escaped when I thumbed her nipple again. She rolled towards me, her eyes opening, blue and hazy from sleep with the desire in them obvious. She cleared her throat, her lips parting and her tongue swiping across the bottom. If she meant to say something, she didn't. She lifted her hand, cupping my cheek and tracing her thumb along my jaw.

Moving on instinct, I shifted so she could roll onto her back and then dipped my head and fit my lips over hers. Fuck me. I could've kissed her for days. The moment our tongues tangled, our kiss went wild—wet, rough, and needy.

I shoved her T-shirt up, dragging it over her head, only tearing my lips away long enough to get her bare underneath me. Groaning at the feel of her silky skin against mine, warm from sleep, I finally broke free of our kiss, blazing a wet path down her neck and into the valley between her breasts. Cupping them both, I laved my tongue over one and then the other, savoring her soft cries and the flex of her body into mine.

Mapping my way down, dropping kisses all over her soft belly, I knew exactly where I meant to bury my mouth next. But she shifted up onto her elbows, nudging me away. I forgot how strong she was. I certainly forgot how quick she was. In a matter of seconds, she had me flat on my back and was straddling me.

Glancing up, my mouth went dry, my heart hammering hard and fast. Susannah was fucking glorious, her strawberry blonde hair catching glints of gold from the sun through the windows, her full breasts with her nipples dusky pink and taut, damp from my attentions. Freckles were scattered here and there on her body, and I loved them, every single one. They were constellations, just hers, and I wanted to map every inch of her, kiss every freckle.

She rolled her hips over my cock, the thin fabric of her panties over my briefs creating a subtle abrasion. My cock throbbed with need. I gripped her hips, but she shook my hands loose, rocking back and catching the waistband of my briefs on her way. She dusted her lips across my chest and over my abdomen, my muscles rippling under her touch. In no time, she freed my cock and shoved my briefs down to my ankles.

Kicking them loose under the sheet, I fell against the pillows. Adjusting them under my head, I looked down. Her hair was a tangle around her face, her cheeks flushed, and her lips swollen from our kisses. Her wide blue eyes caught mine, flashing dark. Her mouth hitched at the corner with a grin as her tongue darted out and she caught a drop of pre-cum running down the length of my cock.

The sight of her, so fucking hot, sent another jolt of need through me and another drop of cum rolling down my shaft. She swirled her tongue around the tip, her eyes on me the whole time. She was so fucking sexy, so fucking hot, I could hardly breathe. Cupping my balls in her hand, she dragged her tongue along one side and then the other of my cock. I meant to watch her, to soak in every minute of this, but I groaned, falling back against the pillows, when she drew me into her wet mouth. With her tongue making me mad, swirling along the base of my cock, her hand fisted around me with wet strokes, she sucked me off like nobody ever had.

My release was thundering through me faster than I wanted as she drew me in and out, pumping my cock. "Zanna... I need to be inside of you. Now," I growled.

"That's what you want?"

Lifting my head with effort, I met her gaze, her eyes dark with need and a wicked glint flickering in their depths. As if she knew how much power she had over me. At my nod, she drew her tongue along my cock once more before rising up, kicking her panties off and straddling me.

She was soaked with desire, her slippery folds sliding back and forth over my cock. I was so close to my release, I had to grip her hips and hold her still.

"Inside," I said. A single word, more of an order than a request.

With her eyes flashing, she rose up, reaching for my cock. She eased down, and it took all of my discipline not to take control. The head of my cock was inside the entrance to her throbbing channel, its heat calling to me. She looked up then, her eyes locking with mine as she slowly sank down over me, taking every inch of me.

When I was fully buried inside of her, she held still and

then began to move, slowly drawing up and rolling her hips down. I didn't know how much longer I could hold out, not with the sight of her above me—her breasts jutting forward, her nipples hard and damp, her belly soft with just a hint of roundness to it now, and her lush bottom held in my hands.

Dear God, I could've come just looking at her. I reached my thumb in between us, pressing down over her clit and growling when she cried out and started to tremble around my cock. At the sound of her calling my name, I let go, my climax thundering through me.

Susannah fell against me, her head tucking into the dip at my neck and shoulder and her breath gusting against my skin. I held her tight, my arms wrapped around her. I could've stayed there forever, buried deep inside of her, my need temporarily slaked.

No such luck though. After a few moments when we both caught our breath, she slowly straightened, her palms resting on my chest. Opening my eyes, I found her looking out the window. I took the moment to simply enjoy the view of her—her checks were flushed, her hair tousled, and her skin was pink all over. My heart gave a squeeze, tightening in my chest. I didn't know what to do with the feelings she elicited. All I knew was everything was getting tangled into everything else.

Every time I thought about her, the next thought would be... *We're having a baby.* I wanted to understand my feelings better, but I didn't know how to separate them. It was becoming more and more clear that I wanted her because of who she was. Every time I tried to imagine letting her go if we weren't having a baby, the answer was resounding. I couldn't even fathom it.

She turned away from the window, catching me watching her. Something flickered in her gaze, but she gave her head a little shake. "We should shower."

Chapter Twenty-Three
SUSANNAH

"When's your next doctor's appointment?"

I was in the middle of pouring hot water into a mug and promptly splattered water all over the counter, startled and distracted by Ward's question.

"Shit," I muttered, snagging a sponge from the sink and quickly wiping up the spilled water.

The moment bought me some time to school my expression to calm. I hadn't meant to wake up beside Ward this morning. I had told myself last night I was going to behave like a rational person and not a sex crazed pregnant woman. I honestly couldn't have told you if I was sex crazed because I was pregnant, or because of Ward. Given the fact I'd never been pregnant before now, I had nothing for comparison there. If I were being honest with myself, I could admit the depth of my attraction to Ward reached levels of power I had never experienced before.

I was out of my mind with need, and I was pregnant. I made a mental note to ask Dr. Jenkins about that, and then immediately ordered myself to scratch that note. Because that would be kind of embarrassing. Like what would I say?

Do women normally want to fuck like rabbits when they're pregnant?

The unflappable Dr. Jenkins would probably take it in stride, but it would be close to mortifying for me. My thoughts looped back to Ward's question. I'd told myself I was going to leave this ball in Ward's court. I didn't want to have expectations, and a big part of me wished I hadn't even mentioned the appointments. Yet, it would be more of a *thing* now if I tried to backtrack, so I elected to play it cool.

Despite my best intentions, I couldn't resist him this morning because...well, just because. I couldn't have stopped myself if the world had been on fire. Well, I suppose the world was on fire when it came to Ward and me.

Once the spill was cleaned up, I rinsed the sponge in the sink and dried my hands, finally ready to face him. I finished filling my cup of tea, contemplating how his question had startled me. Ward had taken the ball and tossed it right back to me. Well, maybe that wasn't fair. I'd asked him if he wanted to go to a doctor's appointment with me. Now, like a normal human being, he was asking when my next appointment was scheduled.

Taking a sip of my tea, I turned around to face him. A good sip of coffee at a stressful moment could get me through most situations, although tea didn't have the same kick. I'd have to make do. "Hang on let me check my card," I managed, my tone remarkably normal sounding given I was a mess inside over one simple question.

I stepped to him where he stood leaning against the counter and handed him the cup of coffee I'd poured for him before I spilled water everywhere. I pulled the card with my appointments out of my purse and returned to the counter where he was sipping his coffee. Catching his eyes, I wasn't sure how to read his expression.

How about you stop over-analyzing everything he does? Unless you want to look as crazy as you are inside.

With a mental eye roll, I slid the card across the counter

to him. Surprisingly, he reached for his phone, spinning it around and quickly entering the entire list of my next three appointments into his phone calendar.

I took another sip of tea and then another, trying to collect myself and figure out what to say. It shouldn't be such a big deal. But then none of this was normal.

It was supposed to be another one night stand. A rather ill conceived one night stand since I'd known this time we were going to see each other again. A lot. It had morphed from that into me being pregnant, and now I was having far more than one night with him. From what I could tell, Ward intended to be involved in our baby's life. I didn't know how I felt about that. I'd have far preferred this to be a clean, no-strings attached situation. A baby was the opposite of no-strings attached. I had to keep reminding myself that I could keep my distance emotionally.

"So does this mean you want to come to an appointment?" I finally asked.

He slid the card across the counter to me. I looked down at the card as though it could somehow give me some answers. Another sip of tea and then I hooked my foot on the leg of the stool closest to me, dragging it close enough to sit down.

Ward's gaze was considering as he stared at me. My stomach was churning, and for a moment, I wondered if I was going to throw up. Oh shit. I was definitely going to throw up. I dashed to the downstairs bathroom, reaching the toilet just in time.

I retched into the toilet and felt his hands brushing my hair back from my neck. I didn't know if it was possible for something to be more undignified than kneeling by the toilet and vomiting in front of the sexiest man you'd ever known.

Ward was rather matter fact about the whole thing. He helped me stand, wet a washcloth for me and handed it over when I swatted his hands away. After dabbing at my face with a cool cloth and rinsing my mouth with water and mouthwash, I returned to the kitchen.

"Morning sickness?" he asked.

I felt like an idiot. I'd had a few bouts of feeling queasy, but this was the first time that I'd actually thrown up. "I guess so," I said with a sheepish laugh.

His eyes crinkled at the corners with a smile. God, I loved it when he smiled. By nature, he was a serious man. He had the whole tall, dark, and dangerous thing going on big time, which only made his rare smiles that much more delectable.

"I don't think I had a chance to answer your question. If it's okay with you, I'll come to all the appointments," he said, as calm as ever.

As if it wasn't completely insane that I was pregnant, we hadn't planned on any of this, and now, apparently, he wanted to come to all of my appointments. Oh well, oh hell.

I stared at him, my mind stumbling over my thoughts. Part of me was crazy happy about this, while another part of me thought it was fucking crazy. Layered on top of that was the part of me that was annoyed at the happy side. It was a three-way argument inside my own head. Sweet Jesus. When I didn't say anything, his smile faded.

"I thought you wanted me to come since you asked."

My head was bobbing up and down like a wild woman. "I asked! It's great you want to come. I just wasn't sure you would want to. Of course it's fine."

He shrugged. "I do."

There was so much more I should probably say, like maybe put the brakes on this madness. But, I had to throw up again.

Chapter Twenty-Four
SUSANNAH

A few days later, I met Lucy for lunch at Firehouse Café. I ordered tea again instead of coffee because my doctor suggested I cut back on coffee. Who knew this would be such a challenge? Armed with my tea and my favorite blueberry scone, I waited for Lucy to arrive.

Lucy was one of several friends I might grab a bite with here and there. Today, I needed advice. If anyone could give it to me, Lucy could.

Within a few minutes, the bell above the door jingled, and I glanced over to see Lucy walking in. I smiled the moment I saw her. She was so gorgeous with her almost fairy-like features—fine-boned and just plain beautiful. Not that she gave a damn. She worked in construction and dressed for her job. Today, she was sporting a pair of overalls over a fitted T-shirt. Her blonde hair was stuffed up into a baseball cap, and a streak of dirt on her cheek completed her look.

After ordering her coffee, she headed my way. Slipping into the chair across from me, she graced me with a wide smile.

"Hey! Amelia and I were just saying we haven't seen you in a couple weeks. You missed our last girls' night."

"I know, I was out at a training that day. Next one, I promise. Is it next week?"

At her nod, I smiled. "I'll be there. Anyway, how are things?"

"Same, same," she said with a smile. "We've been busy with the garage for Levi's dad, and now Levi wants to do an addition on our house because he thinks we should have three bedrooms."

"Why?" I asked.

She sighed, her cheeks cresting pink. "We're talking about kids."

"Perfect. If you want them, do it now. No sense in waiting."

Lucy rolled her eyes. "Easy for you to say."

I cocked my head to the side. "Why do you say it like that?"

"Because you always have life figured out," she said simply. "It took me forever just to figure out how to even admit I was in love with Levi and now he wants to talk about kids. My childhood sucked. What if I'm a terrible mother?"

Reaching across the table, I curled her hand into mine. "You're not going to be a terrible mother. There are no guarantees with anything, but you and Levi are great together, and you'll make great parents."

Lucy sighed again. "Fine. Let me be nervous about it and then I'll figure it out. Anyway, what's up with you?"

There was no way she could've known how on point her topic was. Yet, I still had to muster up the nerve to talk. Somehow, a sip of tea wasn't quite as fortifying as a sip of coffee. "Well, I guess I'll cut to the chase. Speaking of having kids, I'm pregnant."

Lucy promptly spit out her sip of coffee. Handing her a napkin, my cheeks felt hot, but I pushed through. "Trust me, I'm as surprised as you," I offered.

"How? When? Oh my God, what the hell is going on? I feel like I've walked into the twilight zone. Did I miss something? When did you get a boyfriend?"

At her jumble of questions, I shrugged. "Remember that guy Ward I mentioned?"

Her eyes widened. "Oh yeah. Ward was the guy you had the one night stand with, and he was moving here. You were all weird about him."

"Right. Him. Well, it's more than a one night stand now. A bit ago, he was here, and then he had to go back to be with his mom because she was sick. Well..."

I paused and rubbed my face, tunneling my hands into my hair. Saying it aloud made me realize how crazy the whole situation was. Resting my chin in my hands, I looked over at Lucy. Her eyes were wide, but she was patiently waiting. "We decided to have another night, but it was just going to be a one time thing, right?"

Being the gracious friend she was, Lucy nodded along.

"Well, even though we used condoms, I, um, I got pregnant."

"Wasn't this like over a month ago now?" she asked.

"Uh, over six weeks to be exact. How do you know how long he's been here?" I countered.

Lucy rolled her eyes, casting an annoyed look at me. "In case you forgot, I'm married to one of the guys at the station. Levi mentioned the new superintendent was delayed for a month. So this happened six weeks ago and you never even mentioned it to us?"

"Lucy, I'm sorry. I don't..."

She cut in. "Hey, you don't answer to me. Sorry. Sometimes I get all caught up in this whole small town thing," she offered with a wry smile. "I'm as private as you and now I'm worried, so..."

This time, I cut her off. "I get it. I do. I would've gotten around to talking about it, but I didn't think it was a thing. A few weeks ago, I found out I was pregnant, and I've been freaking out since then. To make matters worse, I can't keep my hands off of him. It's a real problem. And now he wants to go to the doctor with me," I said with something close to a wail.

Lucy reached over, this time curling her hand over mine. "Slow down. Okay, I'm caught up. You're freaking yourself out. Don't forget to breathe."

"Okay, okay," I said, nodding quickly. I forced myself to pause and take a deep breath. "I don't know what the hell to do."

"Let's start with the basics. So it sounds like you want to have the baby?"

"Yes. Yes, I do. I didn't plan this, and I'm kinda worried I'm crazy, but I do. I can't imagine not having my baby. I know it's crazy because I don't really know what's going on with Ward and me. But he knows I'm pregnant, and he seems okay with it. I just..." My words ran out and tears pricked at the backs of my eyes. I took a shuddering breath, but I couldn't seem to get enough air into my lungs.

Lucy handed me a napkin, her gaze soft. "Just breathe. It's okay. Slow down. This is definitely one of those times where the whole 'take it one step at a time' is *really* important."

Lucy talked me through it, basically making me give her a blow by blow of everything that happened between Ward and me. I wasn't embarrassed to tell her, but I kept the details *very* light. I mean, I wasn't going to tell her how crazy hot our sex was. I didn't mind admitting I couldn't keep my hands off of him. Hell, trying to pretend otherwise was such a blatant lie, I couldn't quite pull it off.

After she heard the whole messy story, she squeezed my hand again, looked me in the eye and said, "You're just gonna have to figure out what you want."

"What the hell? I thought you would give me advice here."

Lucy's gaze never wavered. "That *is* my advice. You seem

to have decided this is just a casual sex thing. Fine. But a baby isn't casual. A baby is *way* serious. Plus, Ward's actions seem to be saying he wants to be a part of this. To me, that means he's not a total ass. Plenty of guys might get pissed off about an unplanned pregnancy. You're gonna have to set some clear boundaries if you don't want him to take things seriously when it comes to you two. But you can't do this whole avoidance thing. Not about important shit like this. You're having a baby! No matter what, I'm here for you, Amelia's here for you, and Maisie's here for you. You know your parents will move heaven and earth to help you. You are not alone."

I took several sips of my rather unsatisfying tea and a deep breath. "Fine, I'll tell him he needs to understand this isn't more than it is," I muttered.

Lucy nodded and then her eyes took on a gleam. "So, when the hell do we get to meet this guy?"

Chapter Twenty-Five
WARD

I tossed my gear into my locker, snagging a towel and heading into the showers. We had a long afternoon dealing with the fire out at a timber lot. Settling into my role as superintendent with this crew, I was feeling good about it so far. With Chad gone, the rest of the crew was rock solid.

The only issue at the moment was dealing with Susannah's absence. As she'd indicated, she turned in her doctor's recommendation and was taking a planned leave from field duty. Like most stations, Willow Brook Fire & Rescue had light duty options available for crewmembers. She would be handling on site tasks. Conveniently, she could also do work for the police station here, which would keep her from twiddling her thumbs too much.

Rex had arched a brow when he and I spoke about it. He knew something was up, yet he had enough sense to lay low and wait for me to fill him in. Problem was, plenty of the crew had questions about Susannah's status. For now, she seemed to prefer to keep details vague. Yet, Harlow knew she was pregnant, and it wouldn't be too long before that became obvious. At some point she'd have to face it head on. I knew that meant we needed to talk.

Leaning my palms against the cool tile wall, I let the steaming hot water pound down over me. The timber lot this afternoon had been a challenge, but we'd gotten the fire contained. Cade's crew picked up to finish up the job this afternoon. Willow Brook's unique location was a great set up for me to get to know the crew. Often, hotshot crews did nothing but backcountry work. Willow Brook's service to the surrounding areas gave me the opportunity to get to know the crew without being isolated in the middle of nowhere during the process.

Every time my mind shied away from thoughts about Susannah, what she meant to me, and the glaring fact that I was soon to be a father, she was like a boomerang in my brain. As soon as I tried to think about something else, my thoughts swung right back to her and our baby. Snagging the soap, I soaped up and rinsed off and then stood there under the hot water, wishing I could get through to her. Although I might be shaken by it, I didn't doubt how much she meant to me. Yet, I could feel the walls around her.

I felt great when I was with Susannah. Hell, the sex... Out. Of. This. World. I loved falling asleep beside her and waking up beside her. As long as we were tangled up, bare naked, with me buried deep inside of her, I didn't sense those walls she kept up.

The moment that wasn't happening, I could practically see the wheels start turning in her brain and the reinforcements go up around her. With a sigh, I turned off the water and walked past the rest of the guys washing away today's fire. I wasn't much for chatting, although that wasn't particularly unusual. Yet, I needed advice. I couldn't even believe I was thinking that thought. After I was dressed, I snagged a cup of coffee and strolled down the back hallway, relieved to discover Beck was in his office.

Knocking the back of my knuckles against his open door, I waited until he glanced up. "Got a minute?" I asked.

Beck leaned back in his chair where he sat at a small round table in his office. "Of course," he said, waving me in.

Stepping into his office, I nudged the door shut with a heel of my boot. He straightened from where he sat. "Uh oh, is this serious?"

Because it was Beck and he was incapable of resisting the urge to tease, he wagged his eyebrows at me. I shrugged and stepped past his desk. I had no idea why he even bothered with a desk. I'd never seen him sit at it. In fact, it was empty with the exception of a phone. He kept his laptop on the small table where I slipped into a chair across from him.

"I'd offer coffee, but I see you already got some. What's up?" he asked.

On the heels of a deep breath and fortifying sip of coffee, I leaned back in my chair. "Got a question for you."

"Throw it at me."

"So remember how I mentioned Susannah was pregnant?"

"Kinda hard to forget that news bomb," Beck replied with a low chuckle. "I see she put in for light duty. Already hearing questions about what's up with that around the station. I'm sure you are too."

I nodded. "Of course. It'll be up to her to sort out what she wants to say to who and when. Anyway, I could use a little advice. For what it's worth, I can't fucking believe I'm asking for advice. Not really my thing."

Beck flashed his ever-ready grin. "You know me. I love to give advice. Not saying it's worth much though."

"Well, I figure you're my best bet. You're the only guy around I know who's had a baby recently."

Beck's grin shifted from teasing to flat out proud. "Damn straight. Max is great. Having a baby is the best thing we ever did. Also terrifying, seriously terrifying," he said earnestly.

I couldn't help but chuckle. "You don't say?"

His gaze sobered. Closing his laptop, he leaned his elbows on the table, giving me his full attention. "Not sure what you need, but feel free to ask."

Running a hand through my damp hair, I eyed him. "Hell, I don't even know what I need to ask. I guess I need some advice on how to deal with this whole thing. Susannah..." I paused because I didn't quite know how to explain the problem. Whatever, I'd dive straight into it. "If I'm trying to sum it up, it's that I know this is serious for me and Susannah and that has nothing to do with having a baby. But she keeps her distance unless, well, unless we're having sex. I don't know how... Fuck. Basically, I don't know what the hell to do to get her to realize this matters for us."

Beck was quiet, his gaze thoughtful. "Here's the thing, my situation's a little different from yours. I mean, Maisie and I are married. I suppose, a lot of this depends on what the deal is with you and Susannah. Not that I think you guys need to get married. That's a piece of paper. It's more, well, are you a sperm donor? Or a father? Are you serious about her?"

Beck's three questions had been a near mirror of the questions spinning in circles in my mind the last few weeks. Meeting his steady gaze, I took a gulp of coffee and sighed. "Well, I'm definitely not a sperm donor. I didn't plan this, but I'll be a father. I can't imagine having a baby and not being a part of their life. Susannah, well, I can't believe I'm saying this, but I love her. Problem is, every time anything even gets close to serious, she manages to change the subject. It's a damn miracle she asked me to come to the doctor's appointments, and I could tell by the look on her face she wasn't so sure about that either."

"Well, if you love her, tell her."

"Ah, so I'll just tell her that, and it'll all be peaches," I said wryly.

Beck flashed his grin again. "You'd better say something.

Soon. Even though I'd do anything for Maisie and she damn well knows it, she was moody as hell during her pregnancy. Still is. Max is almost three months old now, and she said the other day she's finally starting to feel halfway normal now. Not a hormonal mess. Her words not mine."

Beck eyed me for a long moment. "Look man, I don't know what Susannah wants either. Having a baby is about as serious as it gets. I had to boss Maisie into taking me seriously. I'm sure you'll survive," he offered with a low laugh.

I stared at him and felt myself nodding, but I could hardly think over the rushing sound in my head. It was as if I was caught in a riptide with no choice but to swim through it and hope for the best. I managed to respond to him with some semblance of normal conversation, but I was knocked sideways inside and out.

Leaving Beck's office not much later, I felt even more unsettled than I had before. Because the thing was, I was balancing on a knife's edge with Susannah. My instinct was to demand she face the reality—she belonged to me. Yet, she was so damn independent. I knew in my bones if I got too demanding, she'd push me away. My reaction to that was visceral—my heart clenched and emotion clogged my throat like a vise, nearly choking me.

Possessiveness wasn't something I had experienced before. But with Susannah, the idea of keeping my distance and the reality that might open the door for someone else in her life—ever?

I had one response to that. Hell. No.

Chapter Twenty-Six
SUSANNAH

I dashed through the rain, nudging the door to the grocery store open with my elbow. Throwing the hood on my jacket back once I walked in, I snagged a cart and started making my way through the store. As with basically any moment when I wasn't completely preoccupied, my mind skipped between two tracks – Ward and our baby.

My obsession this morning – whether our baby was a boy or a girl, and how to decide on a name. Oh, and whether or not to include Ward in that decision making process. I also needed to talk to my parents and let them know what was going on. Because my parents were supportive and found a way to cheer me on even when I didn't make the best decisions, I knew they'd be awesome about it, if not a little startled and confused.

I was generally a responsible person. It wasn't like I wanted to explain how wild and crazy that night of sex had been with Ward. Close as I was to both of my parents, that topic was off limits. As with all of my thoughts these days, this train looped right back around to Ward.

Dammit, can't you think of anyone other than him?

No, apparently not.

Topic of the second: when and how to introduce Ward to my parents. And how would I explain him? Did I say he was my boyfriend? Did I say he was an accidental sperm donor? Fuck. I was a mess.

This was the whole problem. Just like Lucy said. I needed to be straight with him.

Rounding the end of one of the aisles, I glanced up when I heard my name. Chad Meyer was standing in front of the beer section, which happened to be right before the egg section. I'd never figure out the rhyme or reason to grocery store organization. But that was the least of my concerns. The last person I wanted to see right now, or at any time for that matter, might've been Chad if I'd given him the favor of taking up space in my mind. Ugh.

Despite all of my mixed feelings about how to deal with Ward as the new superintendent of my crew, he'd proved me right about his leadership by promptly firing Chad. The entire crew had been relieved by his decision.

Ward had been smart about it too. He'd made sure to include Beck and Cade in the decision and in the meeting. Ward, of course, hadn't discussed it with me, nor had I expected that. All of the guys at the station respected Beck and Cade completely. Like myself, they'd also grown up here in Willow Brook. That gave them a level of cachet and respect, if only because everyone at the station knew so much about them and many of the crewmembers had known them for years.

Running into Chad right now? Not exactly what I wanted to deal with. Chad had also been the equivalent of a gnat as far as hitting on me. Rex Masters and Al, our former crew superintendent, had once pulled me aside last year to check in. Chad's pursuit of me had been that obvious. They wanted to make sure I felt okay coming to them if he was a problem.

I'd been fine. Frankly, it had annoyed me to have them

worry I couldn't handle it myself. Looking back, I realized they were only trying to make sure I knew they had my back. Chad had dialed it down after the last time I told him to fuck off, but he never gave up the chase altogether. He struck me as the kind of guy who fed off of anything he perceived as a challenge. By turning him down, I'd unintentionally become a challenge he wanted to beat.

Meeting Chad's flat brown gaze, which always held a hint of anger, I smiled tightly and kept on moving. "Hey Chad," I said casually as I walked past him with my cart.

My cart came to an abrupt, swinging stop when he gripped the side of it quickly. I hadn't been moving that fast, but had just enough momentum going to bump into the cart. Reflexively, I curled my arm over my belly.

Annoyed, I cast my eyes sideways. "Here for a reason Chad, and it's not to socialize."

He smiled, a smile that never quite reached his eyes. "How about dinner?" he asked.

"No." I reached over and tried to knock his hand off, but he didn't budge, only tightening his grip on the side of the cart.

"We don't work together now. No convenient excuse anymore," he said flatly.

"Like I've told you many times before, whether we work together or not, we're not having dinner, we're not having lunch, we're not having breakfast, and we're not doing anything together. Not interested," I said firmly, not even bothering to try to be polite.

Furious, I reached up and gave his knuckles a hard knock. He only tightened his grip again with a grim smile.

"Chad, let go."

I was about to open my mouth again when I felt Ward approaching me from behind. That was how familiar I'd become with Ward. I could sense his presence without even seeing him. Relief washed over me. I wasn't scared of Chad, but he was a fucking asshole, and an entitled asshole to boot.

I might not want to admit that sometimes it was nice to have a man around, but right now it was. Unlike me, Ward was bigger, taller and stronger than Chad.

Ward stopped at my side. His eyes flicked to me briefly and then to Chad. "Pretty sure I just heard her ask you to let go," he said, his voice low with a hint of danger.

Because I was getting quite familiar with how Ward felt, I knew he was furious right now. He was fairly vibrating with fury.

Chad, being the idiot he was, still didn't let go of my cart. He sneered at Ward. "What the hell are you gonna do about it? You're not my boss anymore. Did you forget that?"

Ward's eyes narrowed. He reached over, curled his hand over Chad's arm, his grip closing down. "I didn't forget a thing. Actually, it's better I'm not your boss anymore. I don't have to be professional about this. Get your fucking hands off of her cart and leave her alone."

Ward must've squeezed down hard enough to cause Chad a hint of pain. Chad's cheeks reddened, and he swore as he yanked his hand away.

"Fuck you. Fuck you both. Speaking of fucking, I know you want a piece of that," Chad said, jutting his chin in my direction.

For a flash, I worried Ward would haul off and hit Chad right here in the grocery store. But, he was a controlled man. With his fists balled at his sides and his eyes dark, he simply stated, "Get the hell away from her. Now."

Conveniently, someone turned into the aisle, a mother with three children clustered around her hips. Chad took the opportunity to stride away quickly. Ward watched as he walked away, only turning to me when Chad was out of sight. His eyes coasted over me, the concern contained in his gaze sending my pulse off like a rocket and a curl of warmth around my heart.

"You okay?" he asked.

"Of course. Chad was just being an ass, but then he's

always an ass. We didn't talk about it, but you might want to know the crew's happy you fired him."

Ward simply nodded, his gaze still considering. "Did he ask you out?"

His question startled me. I finally shrugged because it wasn't exactly news that Chad had chased after me last year. "Yeah. He's been on me for about a year. He used to think I was saying no because we worked together. Didn't matter that I told him every single time I wasn't interested."

Ward's eyes darkened—like the sky on a stormy day. Another family turned down the aisle, a little boy running past us and calling out, "Candy!"

Ward curled his hands on the cart handle. "Let's finish shopping."

Although this definitely wasn't the time or place, my mouth seemed to have a mind of its own. "Let's? Let's make one thing clear. I was here shopping. On my own. I can certainly finish by myself."

His gaze was implacable. If he was rattled at all by my comments, it didn't show.

"I'm here now," was all he said.

"And what does that mean?"

That question seemed to pierce him. Narrowing his eyes, he stared at me. After a beat, he replied, "Don't push me away for something as minor as helping you with groceries."

Although a part of me was ready to argue the point, I was suddenly tired. I was too emotionally out of whack to make sense of any of this right now. I just wanted to finish shopping and go home.

Chapter Twenty-Seven
WARD

Unbeknownst to Susannah, I'd ended up at the grocery store when I saw her car in the parking lot. My wheels had practically turned on their own. I just couldn't resist the draw.

Right now, as I stood behind her car unloading groceries into the back, I was fucking furious. Not with her. Rather, I was angry with Chad and with myself. As soon as I turned down that aisle and saw the look on his face, I'd known he was pressuring her again. It had taken most of my discipline not to walk up and clock him in the face.

I was furious with myself because I couldn't fucking control myself when it came to Susannah. Even though I could actually tell myself it was clear she wasn't interested in Chad, I was jealous. Me. Jealous!

Never in my fucking life had I been jealous. Oh, I'd seen assholes hit on women that I dated before and plenty of women I was friends with. My reaction was about the same either way. Back off. But that was it. More of a friendly, leave them the hell alone kind of vibe.

With Susannah? Oh, hell no. That was all that went through my head. That and...

Mine.

Meanwhile, I planned on following her home to help unload the groceries. I sensed she was trying to assess where I was at with things. I knew exactly how I felt, but I would bide my time until she was ready to deal with it.

I generally considered myself a respectful man. I'd never been one of those guys who didn't think women could be hotshot firefighters. Trust me when I tell you, there were plenty of guys like that. Not me. Women were strong, fearless, and often smarter than men in a pinch. Because they didn't have brute strength on their side, they had to think smart.

Never once when I was training with Susannah, or working with any of the other female firefighters I'd worked with, had I felt the need to protect them. No more so than a general sense of wanting to protect anyone I worked with.

But now? With Susannah, I was a fucking caveman. I didn't want her to lift anything heavy. I didn't want her to put herself in danger in any way. Hell, I didn't even want her to be stressed out, not even a little. I supposed I should consider the fact I might be a source of stress for her, what with my simple existence in her life. But that wasn't a place I wanted to go right now.

She looked a little tired, which made sense. I knew precisely what, or rather who, had interfered with her sleep last night. Me. Although she was the one who started it this time.

After closing the hatch on her car, I wheeled the cart to the front of the store. It had started to drizzle after I left the station. When I returned to her car, she was standing at the back with her arms crossed, oblivious to the soft rain falling.

"What are you doing?" she asked

I shrugged. "Helping you unload the groceries at your house."

She actually laughed, shaking her head slowly. "I can handle it, you know."

"So can I," I countered with a grin.

She laughed again, her cheeks flushing. "Fine. I can't seem to say no to you."

Relief rolled through me. Climbing in my truck, I followed her back out to her house, wrestling with my impatience. I wanted to push the point with her.

There was the possessive streak again. I shook my thoughts away, telling myself to give her more time. I soaked in the view as I navigated the short drive outside of downtown Willow Brook. I didn't think I'd ever get tired of the view here. It was late afternoon. Even with the clouds hanging low, Swan Lake was beautiful. Swans had returned for the spring and were floating on its surface. In the distance, the mountains rose through the clouds with Denali rising tall above everything else.

Snow still sat on its peak, and from what I understood, it would be there all summer. Turning down Susannah's driveway, I rolled to a stop beside her car.

In short order, I had carried all the groceries inside, completely ignoring her plea that she could deal with it. Closing the refrigerator, I turned to face her.

She stood by the counter, her hands curled over the edge. Her strawberry hair was damp from the drizzle, and her cheeks were flushed. Damn. She was so fucking beautiful. I ran the math in my head, calculating she was almost eight weeks pregnant now. Emotion rocked me. If I didn't know her body so well by this point, I might not notice the soft curve of her belly. But I did.

If you'd told me it would turn me on to have a woman pregnant with my baby, I'd have told you were flat insane. I'd have been wrong, so very wrong. Whether it was specific to Susannah or not, I had no clue. All I knew was I wanted her like mad.

Stepping to her, I leaned my hands against the counter on either side of her, caging her in my arms. Closing my eyes for a beat, I breathed in the scent of her.

Chapter Twenty-Eight
WARD

Susannah held still for a beat, her body tensing slightly. Lifting my head, my gaze collided with hers—her wide blue eyes with her strawberry blonde lashes brushing against her cheeks. The air around us felt heavy, weighted with the need that vibrated between us whenever we were close to each other.

I was relieved, if only to know she was perhaps as powerfully drawn to me as I was to her. I'd never claim to know what was in her mind. Certainly not what was in her heart. Yet, I knew what I felt physically with her. It was a force of its own, beyond my control.

I'd recognized it four years ago, that single night we shared. That was why I'd given into it. Because I knew its depth and its power, and I wanted a taste of it. Foolishly and arrogantly, I'd thought I had the perfect way to face it without getting drawn too deeply inside its centrifugal force. One night and then we'd never see each other again. Easy. So I'd thought.

For a second time, my arrogance led me into the maelstrom. Here I was now, nearly a slave to my need for Susannah. There was no such thing as enough when it came to her. I doubted I could ever slake my need. It ran deep as a river in my veins, permeating every fiber of my being.

Lifting a hand, I brushed a few loose curls off of her cheek. I even loved the way her hair felt—silky soft with a mind of its own, always curling here and there. She wasn't one to style her hair. Rather, she just let it do its thing, and I loved it. I'd have probably hated if she tried to tidy it. Her hair reminded me of her when she let her guard down – wild and unrestrained.

When I tucked those curls behind her ear, she leaned toward me as my hand slid around to cup her nape. I couldn't *not* touch her when we were this close. My thumb brushed idly along the side of her neck, feeling the rapid beat of her pulse. Another wash of relief rolled through me. Because I couldn't be close to her without my heart beating like a drum. I didn't care to be alone, caught in the storm of desire by myself.

"How are you?" I murmured.

Her eyelids had dropped, and they flicked back up, a slight smile curling the corners of her mouth. Her teeth snagged the side of her bottom lip. Fuck me. Just that simple sight—her teeth denting the plump pillow of her lip, and my cock hardened even further.

"I'm fine," she said with a soft laugh. "I suppose we forgot that part."

Recalling I had forgotten to ask how she was doing earlier and the reason why sent a lingering jolt of fury through me. Chad being a fucking asshole, and my irrational jealousy that any man would notice her. Shaking those thoughts away, I focused on the feel of her close to me, sliding my palm down her spine to palm her lush bottom and arching into the apex between her thighs. The feel of the damp heat there called to me.

"I suppose we did forget. So you're feeling okay? Any more morning sickness?"

Her teeth released her lip, and I was ridiculously disappointed. I was so attuned to everything about her, my responses were heightened.

She shook her head slightly. "Nope, just a little queasy here and there. How are you?"

I'd almost lost focus, what with her pressed against me, her warm, lush curves right there. Lifting a shoulder in a shrug, I replied, "Fine. Other than Chad being an ass."

With a roll of her eyes, she shook her head slightly. "I can deal with him. He's not from around here, so I'm sure he'll move on soon. Seeing as he can't get work at Willow Brook Fire & Rescue, he doesn't have many options here."

As she spoke, she uncurled a hand from around the edge of the counter, her fingers toying with the buttons on my shirt.

"Are we done with that?" I asked.

"With what?"

"You know, being polite."

Her eyes darkening, she nodded, her tongue darting out to moisten her lips.

"Good," I growled before fitting my mouth over hers and giving in to the need thundering through me with such force I could hardly think.

Chapter Twenty-Nine
SUSANNAH

In a matter of seconds, I was burning up inside. That was how enslaved I was to my body and to the need I simply could not deny. I couldn't get enough of Ward. I doubted I ever would.

Our tongues tangled in a hot, wet, wild kiss that nearly brought me to my knees. Thank God I was leaning against the counter and Ward was holding me close. I could feel the hard, hot length of his shaft pressing against my lower belly. His hand cupped my bottom, holding me tight against him.

My panties were soaked and had been the entire drive home. All I could think about was getting here and getting naked. In that vein, there were far too many layers between us.

Tearing my lips free from his, I made quick work of the buttons on his shirt. In a rare exception, he wasn't wearing a T-shirt today, but rather a worn, soft flannel button-down. I sighed at the feel of his warm skin under my touch, my hands mapping his chest and trailing down over the rippling muscles of his abdomen.

As I tore at the buttons of his jeans, he made even

quicker work of my blouse. Unlike me, he didn't bother to deal with the buttons. He simply tore at it, buttons pinging on the tile floor in my kitchen. Flicking my eyes up to his, I murmured, "Just ruin my blouse, why don't you?"

Entirely unrepentant, he lifted one of his muscled shoulders in a shrug with a sly grin, his eyes flashing silver. It said something that even a shrug was sexy when Ward did it.

I grinned because I couldn't help it, and then he was lifting me up, yanking my jeans down as he did. Somehow in a matter of seconds, he had all of my clothes off except for my panties. He lifted me up onto the counter behind me, the cool tile a balm to the heat licking through my entire body.

With his mouth on one of my nipples and his thumb teasing the other, I was panting and gasping hoarsely. His teeth scored my nipple lightly, and I cried out, tangling my fingers in his hair. I reached between us, tearing the buttons of his fly open, relieved he didn't bother with briefs or boxers most of the time. The hot velvety skin of his cock felt so good as I curled my palm around it, shoving his jeans down around his hips to gain better access.

"Fuck, Susannah," he murmured. "You make me crazy."

Ward lifted his head, his stormy gaze snagging mine as his hand trailed down over my belly, his fingers dragging across the wet silk between my thighs.

"God, I love how wet you get. How long have you been like this?"

My emotions raw, nothing but need driving me, I answered honestly. "Since I saw you."

His smoky gaze darkened further. He didn't say anything, he simply shoved my panties out of the way and sank two fingers inside me, knuckle deep. I was so wet and so ready, I whimpered in relief. But it wasn't enough. I needed him filling me, stretching me, making me forget everything but him and the connection between us.

"I need you," I gasped.

He didn't hesitate, stepping back slightly. He gripped his cock in his fist and dragged it through my folds, coating it in my juices. His eyes caught mine again. "You want this?"

Sensation was flying through me, sparks scattering through my entire body. I felt molten inside and out. Unable to tear away from his gaze or to form words, I merely nodded, rocking my hips toward him. He dragged his cock up and down again, teasing over my slippery wet clit.

"You're going to have to say it."

"Yes," I finally cried out, somehow managing to form that one single word with my lips.

"Watch," he ordered.

Only then did he break his gaze free of mine, looking down between us. I simply did as he asked, my eyes following his. His cock was a thing of beauty—hard and thick, glistening from my desire. Without even a hint of self-consciousness, he slid his fist up and down his cock as I watched. A drop of pre-cum rolled out of the tip, falling onto my belly.

I didn't know how it was physically possible to need him more, but I did. That simple sight nearly pushed me over the edge, my channel clenching and throbbing.

"Ward, please. I need you."

"Right here," he murmured.

I became the demanding one, ordering him. "I need you inside me. Now."

"All you had to do was ask," he growled as he sank into me.

Crying out, I arched back as he gripped my hips, pulling me closer to the edge of the counter. He held still, and I sighed at the feel of the delicious stretch of him filling me completely.

"Susannah."

Managing to drag my eyes open, I found his gaze waiting. My heart gave a hard thump. The moment was so intense and so intimate, I could hardly bear it. Yet, I did. Because with his eyes there and his body surrounding me, I felt safe.

After holding still for a few beats, he finally drew his hips back. He set a steady rhythm, drawing back and sinking in—again and again, a slow pull and slide. I was so drenched, so overcome with need, it was only a few strokes and then I flew apart, pleasure crashing over me with a wave so hard and intense, I lost sight of everything but Ward and the feel of him.

Distantly, I heard myself crying his name repeatedly. Amidst the aftershocks of my own pleasure, I felt his body tighten and then the heat of his release pouring into me with a final surge. Savoring my name on his lips, I watched as he lost control.

His head fell to my shoulder, his breath gusting against my skin. We stayed like that with me held tight in his embrace. I didn't want to ever move and probably wouldn't have were it not for the chill that raced through me eventually.

Ward lifted his head, his eyes catching mine. Without a word, he stepped back, easily lifting me in his arms and carrying me into the shower with him.

I was getting too comfortable with this, yet I liked it too much to try to create any distance just now.

Chapter Thirty
WARD

Sitting in the doctor's office, I rested my elbows on my knees and resisted the urge to twist my hands together. Damn. This was an entirely new experience for me. Glancing around the small examination room, I took in the space. There was a table, on which Susannah currently sat, with crinkly white paper on it and those foot stirrups that men only heard about.

Well, unless they were an expectant father and attending one of these appointments. Beyond the table, there was a counter behind it with a small sink, a giant bottle of disinfectant and boxes of what I imagined to be all kinds of medical odds and ends. The walls were covered with posters about what to expect at different stages of pregnancy. Aside from the chair I currently occupied, there was a stool on wheels with an attached table. The entire space felt sterile and chilly.

Susannah sat on the table in a thin cotton gown that tied behind her neck. Her legs were bare, but she'd kept her socks on, which was strangely endearing. At the moment, her feet were swinging back and forth idly. Her eyes flicked to mine and then away before she brushed a loose lock of hair away from her face, tucking it behind her ear.

"What's your doctor's name?" I asked.

"Dr. Jenkins."

"How well do you know her?"

I suddenly had a host of questions about Susannah's doctor, none of which were likely any of my business. Yet, this was the doctor who was overseeing her pregnancy. I suddenly cared. A lot.

Susannah's gaze caught mine again, and she rolled her eyes. "She's been my doctor since I was a teenager. It's fine for you to be here, but don't go thinking I would change doctors if you asked. I trust her, and I'm comfortable with her," she said firmly.

I couldn't help but chuckle. It was as if she'd read my mind. Not that I'd been planning to ask her to change doctors, but it was important for her to have a good doctor.

"I wouldn't consider it," I finally managed.

"Liar," Susannah retorted with a grin.

At that moment, the door to the examination room opened, and Dr. Jenkins stepped through. She wore a white lab coat, as expected, with her name embroidered on it in purple lettering. Her dark hair was pulled back in a tight twist with streaks of silver shot through it. She wore glasses and had sharp brown eyes.

"Hello Susannah," she said with a slight smile. "I understand from Jane in reception that you have company today." Her gaze spun to me, her eyes far too perceptive for my comfort. She turned, stepping to me and holding out her hand. "Dr. Jenkins."

I stood and reached out to shake her hand. She shook hands like she spoke, strong and firm. Everything about her screamed matter-of-fact and no-nonsense.

It suddenly occurred to me that she might care that Susannah's baby was the product of what was supposed to have been a one night stand. I hoped it counted for something that I was here.

Once I was standing, I didn't quite know what to do with myself and stuffed my hands in my pockets after Dr. Jenkins released my hand. It only belatedly occurred to me I hadn't returned her introduction. If that didn't tell you how fucked up I was inside my head, I didn't know what would.

"Ward, Ward Taylor," I offered belatedly.

When my eyes flicked to Susannah, her cheeks were pink. It occurred to me she might be just as uncomfortable with this as I was. Not for the first time, I wished I knew how to navigate this.

Dr. Jenkins simply nodded with a friendly smile and turned to start checking on Susannah. Meanwhile, my mind wandered off temporarily.

See the thing was, I had no idea how to do this. I knew exactly what I wanted, but Susannah's walls weren't making it easy. I could fight fires, save lives, lift all kinds of heavy things... Yet, fighting to get Susannah to accept she was meant to be mine. Well, not so easy. Even while I was confident in what I wanted, it didn't help that I had no experience to speak of.

My own father didn't hang around too long. He managed the sperm donor part just fine. He'd also set himself up quite well in the divorce from my mother. I supposed it had been smart to marry into money. That was round one of father role models for me.

Role model two was my stepfather, Dwight's father. He'd thought he was smart by marrying into money. But my mother wasn't so foolish anymore. She hadn't been so cynical as to avoid marriage altogether, but she was quite practical about the money side of things by then. My stepfather had also managed the sperm donor part just fine. Dwight came along and then when he was about five, my stepfather filed for divorce. He got his divorce, but no money. He proceeded to spend the next twelve years or so giving my mother hell, taking her back to court again and again in one failed effort after another to finagle money out of her. Poor Dwight had to bounce back and forth between his dad and my mom. It was no wonder he was a mess inside about who and what mattered in his life.

In short, as far as learning how to be a father, my skills were limited, but I'd be damned if I'd let any child of mine grow up without a father who was very involved in their life.

Now my mother, she'd been amazing. She was a rock for me and for Dwight. I didn't know if he would ever admit it, but the choice she made to never badmouth his father was a gift. She was there for us in every way that mattered. Dwight tied it all into money, while I would've given the world to have more time with her.

No such luck. I figured if I could be half as good of a father as my mother had been a mother, I might be halfway decent.

My meandering train of thought was interrupted when Dr. Jenkins said my name.

"Ward?" Her tone indicated she'd said my name more than once already.

I looked her way and nodded. "Sorry about that." My next words surprised me. "I've never been to anyone else doctor's appointment. It's a little strange."

Dr. Jenkins' smile felt more than polite this time. She nodded her head towards the screen behind the examination table. While I'd been zoning out, she had Susannah laying down on the table and something between her legs. I didn't dare ask what it was.

Dr. Jenkins gestured to the screen. "There's your baby."

Staring at the screen, I saw a grainy black, white, and gray image with the distinct shape of a baby curled up. Stunned speechless, I simply stared at it. When I didn't say anything, Dr. Jenkins carried on. "So that sound you hear..." She paused looking at me, a brow raised in question. I nodded when I heard a rushing sound and a faint, but steady thump underneath it. "That's the heartbeat," she finished.

With my heart tight, I stared. I had tons of questions. I limited myself to one. "When will we know if it's a boy or a girl?"

"I've already scheduled the next ultrasound. That'll be at roughly twenty-one weeks. We should be able to tell then."

I met her steady, kind gaze and managed to nod. Emotion rocked me, kicking at my heart and clogging in my throat. I looked down to Susannah where she lay in her thin gown, my eyes distantly noticing she had goose bumps and her skin had a chilled, bluish hue to it.

For a moment, it was as if we were alone in the sterile room. Dr. Jenkins' presence faded. Our eyes met and that now familiar electricity arced to life between us.

At that moment, Dr. Jenkins' beeper went off, the sound snapping through the intimacy. I looked away, but slid my hand on Susannah's calf.

Dr. Jenkins stepped away to answer her pager, asking Susannah to hold the wand.

"The wand?" I asked once Dr. Jenkins was out of earshot.

Susannah grinned, the paper underneath her crinkling as she shifted to reach between her thighs. "This thing," she said, wiggling it. "Trust me, you have no idea how lucky you are to be a man. You might think this is fun, but it's not. It's a cold, hard wand. It's what they use for the ultrasound," she explained when I still looked confused.

"Oh," I finally said just as Dr. Jenkins stepped back into the room.

Dr. Jenkins got right back to business, quickly reviewing a few things, spelling out everything for me. Once she declared she was done, she calmly had Susannah remove the wand, quickly taking off the condom on it and tossing it in the waste basket nearby, along with her latex gloves. I stood there, contemplating how it had never occurred to me a condom would be used in a doctor's office.

After Susannah was sitting up, Dr. Jenkins glanced between us. "Any more questions?"

I looked to Susannah because I really had no idea what to ask. I didn't quite think it would be appropriate if I asked Dr. Jenkins how to persuade Susannah what lay between us was so much more than sex.

Driving home later that afternoon, I was impatient. After we left the doctor's office, Susannah got distant again. She didn't even give me a chance to get close enough to kiss her and practically ran to her car. I was reaching the point where I wanted to demand more, to force her to face what was so obvious.

Chapter Thirty-One
SUSANNAH

My mother stared at me, her eyes wide. I'd inherited her eyes—sky blue and almost translucent. I also had her hair. I'd hated my hair color when I was younger. It was just strawberry enough I'd gotten tagged with the occasional nickname *Red*. Even now as an adult, I didn't quite understand who came up with the term strawberry blonde.

But my hair color wasn't really the point right now. I'd done the impossible. I'd shocked my mother.

"You're pregnant?" she asked.

"Uh huh. I know it's a surprise. I was surprised too."

We were in the kitchen at my parents' house. Their house was on a bluff overlooking a field with the mountains in the distance. I supposed you could say 'with the mountains in the distance' to describe almost any location in Alaska. Yet, despite its commonality here, it didn't change the stunning beauty.

I loved my parents' kitchen, probably because I spent so much time here growing up. They lived in a farmhouse style home with the kitchen to match. Cabinets lined the walls with a massive island with the stovetop and a sink in the middle and stools surrounding it. This had been my homework station when I was growing up. My mother used to cook dinner while I did my homework.

Before my announcement, my mother had been busy chopping carrots. I was seated across from her on one of the stools, sipping on a cup of tea. It was a chilly spring afternoon, and my hands were cold. I curled them around the warm mug, absorbing its heat.

Setting down her chopping knife, she reached for a stool on the corner of the counter. Pulling it towards her, she sat down. "Well, I'm guessing you wouldn't be telling me this if you weren't planning on having a baby," she finally said.

"I am. Maybe it's crazy, and I sure as hell didn't plan on this, but it's happening."

My mother nodded slowly, the surprise gradually fading from her expression. "I hope you don't mind me asking who the father is. I wouldn't ask, except I don't even know if you're seeing anyone."

She looked apologetic. As close as I was to my mother, she wasn't a nosy person. In general, she let me have my space and waited for me to come to her.

"Of course you can ask. It wasn't serious before. But I suppose we're moving in that direction now. It's Ward, Ward Taylor."

My mother's eyes widened. "The new superintendent for your crew?"

At my nod, her eyes widened even further. I decided to go ahead and address all the questions I imagined she had. "Mom, I met him years ago in training in California. We didn't have anything serious, but... Well, we had a thing. He came back, and you don't need to tell me it wasn't the best plan to get involved with my boss, but I did."

My cheeks were hot. I might not have said it out loud, but my point was rather obvious.

My mother grinned slyly. "I see."

"Not that I want to get into all the details, but before

you go thinking we were irresponsible, we used condoms. I got pregnant anyway. I wasn't sure how Ward would handle the news, but he's been great about it. I haven't talked to you about it sooner, because, well... I was pretty freaked out about it."

"How far along are you?"

"Ten weeks."

My mother stared at me, her mouth dropping open before she snapped it shut. "How long have you known?"

"About a month for sure. I just needed some time to get used to the idea before I talked to anybody about it. I hope you understand," I said, knowing it probably hurt her to realize I'd kept the news to myself. By pure chance, I'd only seen her once since I knew. Usually I'd see my parents every week or so, but they'd been out of town for a trip to visit some friends in Washington for two weeks out of the month.

After a few moments of silence, she cocked her head to the side and smiled slowly. "Once your Dad gets used to the idea, he's going to be ecstatic. I don't suppose we'll get to meet Ward soon, will we?"

"Of course you will. I wanted to talk to you first and then I need to talk to him."

My mother's perceptive gaze coasted over me. "Are you two serious now?"

All of a sudden, tears pricked hot at the backs of my eyes. Because I didn't know what we were. I could feel the frustration emanating from Ward. He wasn't the kind of man to hold back. Yet, my own frustration was building. I wanted our baby, but I felt boxed in by the situation and too easily swayed by my body. The fire between us burned too hot to ignore, but it would have made it so much easier if I didn't want him the way I did.

Since the doctor's appointment, he continued to spend every night with me. Every night, we had crazy, hot sex. Because that was all we seemed to know how to do. But when we weren't tangled up, nearly two fused as one, I didn't know how to handle his presence in my life. I wanted to push him away and pull him close at once. I knew I could be stubborn, but I wasn't used to feeling caught in the storm of circumstance and hormones.

I didn't realize I had started to cry until my mother handed me a tissue. She was quiet for a moment and then shocked the hell out of me. "You were a surprise."

"I was?" I asked, looking up at her as I knuckled another tear rolling down with the tissue balled in my fist.

She nodded, smiling softly. "Oh, I was head over heels in love with your father by that point, but we weren't even engaged then. I was on birth control, but every so often I'd forget to take it. That's how I got pregnant with you. You were the best accident that ever happened to me. By the time I realized I was pregnant, I was eight weeks along. Because, you see, I didn't have much of a period with the pill, so I didn't notice anything amiss until I started throwing up every morning."

I burst out laughing because it was all so ridiculous. "So when did you and dad decide to get married?"

"Oh hon, you already know that. He asked me right away and then we eloped."

Hope tried to catch my attention, waving a little flag in my heart. It all seemed so simple—if only I could believe Ward wasn't just doing this out of obligation.

I had heard that part of my parents' story, but somehow I'd missed the part that I was a surprise. When I said as much, my mother shrugged.

"It wasn't important. I don't know what's between you and Ward, and I certainly haven't met him so I have nothing to go on." She paused, her perceptive gaze scanning my face. "It sounds like he's stepping up. That's a good thing, right?"

Oh God. My mom had an opinion. I could practically feel her biting her tongue. It wasn't like I could tell her I was sex crazed and couldn't think straight because of it. It almost annoyed me that Ward was so, well, *there* for me.

"Of course it is. It's just. I don't know. Even though I want my baby, I'm not so sure it's a great plan to make decisions about us as a couple on short notice like this. We aren't like you and Dad were. I mean..."

My mother shook her head sharply. "Hon, life throws curve balls all the time. Sure, it's easy to say that because your father and I were already together when I got pregnant that it was meant to be. But that's not how it works. Every relationship, especially one that includes a child, requires work. I make a choice every day to keep working on what I have with your father. He does the same. You can't coast on the fun, crazy beginning of any relationship. It's not that simple. You build your own foundation. I'm not saying you have to be with Ward. I'm just saying don't go looking for something to tell you its meant to be. Some people create amazing marriages out of accidents. Others plan everything within an inch of their lives and blow their marriage to pieces. You have to roll with life and ride the waves instead of fighting against them. If Ward is committed and he's there for you and the baby, well that says a lot about him."

After that little speech, about all I could do was nod. I wasn't ready for more yet.

Chapter Thirty-Two
SUSANNAH

"Again?" Lucy asked, her voice disbelieving.

Amelia laid her cards on the table with a roll of her eyes. "Why do you look so surprised? Maisie almost always wins."

Leaning back in my chair, I glanced to Maisie who merely shrugged. "You can't expect me to throw a game just because you want to win," she offered with a sly grin.

Lucy rolled her eyes and reached over to lift the bottle of wine from the middle of the table. Filling her wine glass, she sighed. "Fine. I can always be hopeful. Every once in a while someone else wins."

Lucy's gaze caught mine as Amelia leaned over to snag the wine bottle from her. Without saying a word, I knew she was wondering when I planned to share my news with everyone.

It wasn't that I was trying to keep it a secret anymore, but more that I was trying to figure out the best timing. Amelia promptly offered me an easy in when she glanced my way, starting to hand me the wine bottle before setting it down. "Where's your wine glass?"

I wasn't a heavy drinker, but I generally enjoyed a glass of wine or beer with my friends. I met her gaze and shrugged. "I guess now is as good a time as any. I'm pregnant."

My last two words dropped with a thud in the middle of the table. We were having our girls' night. It was nothing official, but we regularly got together to play cards, have dinner, and just hang out. Tonight, we were at Cade and Amelia's place. Cade had been shooed off to catch a beer with the guys at Wildlands.

We were seated at a small round table in their kitchen. Amelia had built this place a few years before Cade moved back to Willow Brook. The downstairs was open and airy with the kitchen at the back opening into the living room. Glancing around the table, I had two startled pairs of eyes on me between Amelia and Maisie. Amelia glanced to Lucy who didn't look as surprised because I'd already told her I was pregnant.

"How come you don't look shocked?" Amelia asked.

I answered for Lucy. "Because I already told her. I needed some advice."

"You're pregnant?" Maisie asked, her tone disbelieving.

"Uh huh," I said, feeling my cheeks heat. "I suppose I'd better explain it all. So four years ago, I met Ward at training in California. Never thought I'd see him again. So we had a one-night stand. No big deal right?" Glancing around the table, I met the still wide eyes of Amelia and Maisie and a look of empathy from Lucy. I continued, "So when he showed up here..."

Maisie cut in. "He's your boss."

My cheeks got even hotter. "Tell me something I don't know. Anyway, I guess you could say there was still some chemistry. It was supposed to be just another night. But I got pregnant. So now..." I sighed, resting my chin in my hands and glancing around at my friends. "Well, now I'm having a baby."

Maisie's eyes coasted over me. "I noticed you looked a little different. If I'd known, I would've figured it out right away. But since you haven't even been dating anyone, at least not that I knew, I certainly wasn't wondering if you were pregnant. Tell me, how far along are you?"

On the heels of another deep breath, I answered, "Almost at the end of my first trimester, ten and a half weeks."

Amelia's mouth dropped open. "How long have you known?"

"Well, I did a pregnancy test the week after I missed my period, so about five weeks. Look, I was pretty freaked out about it and still am. I waited to confirm it with my doctor and then I talked to Ward."

"So are you two official?" Maisie asked.

I'd asked myself that same question again and again and again. Emotion tightened in my chest, but I ignored it. "I don't know," I finally said.

"What about him? How does he feel about the baby? Because a baby is kind of a big deal," Maisie said.

"Obvious much?" Lucy asked.

Maisie rolled her eyes. Collecting the cards scattered on the table, she looked over to me. "I wasn't being sarcastic. Beck and I wanted to have a baby, and it's still so much more work than I ever could've imagined. I wouldn't change it for a second, but it's no joke."

"I know. I didn't plan this, and I'm probably crazy, but it's happening."

Amelia took a gulp of her wine, her gaze somber as she looked over at me. "And you're sure this is what you want?"

"Trust me, I know I have options. But this is what I want. I know it doesn't make sense. It wasn't like we were careless about it. We used condoms. They just didn't work."

Lucy burst out laughing at that. "I'd say not. How are things with Ward?"

The emotion I could never seem to swat away tightened in my chest again. "I think things are okay," I finally managed.

"Have you decided what you want?" she asked, referencing her simple advice to me earlier.

Amelia glanced between Lucy and me. "Obviously, you two had a chat. Let me guess, you figured Lucy would give you the most blunt advice."

Grinning, I nodded. "Of course she did. I just haven't followed it."

"What was it?" Amelia asked.

"Oh, you know, the obvious. I need to figure out what I want. Here's the thing with Ward, the sex is great. I mean like *great, great*. But that kinda makes it hard for me to know how I really feel. I mean..." I paused, trying to gather my thoughts into something that made sense. "I guess I'm worried I'm letting the great sex lead me into something serious when I'm not sure that's what I want. We shouldn't get serious just because I'm pregnant."

Three pairs of eyes stared back at me as I glanced around. Though the expressions varied, the general vibe was *what the hell*.

"Well, how did he deal with the news that you're pregnant?" Maisie finally asked.

"Better than I expected. I mean, he was shocked, but once I told him I was having the baby, he's been... Well I guess he's been supportive."

"I get that you don't want to assume great sex equals a great relationship, but seeing as you've decided you're having a baby and he's the father, this isn't a simple situation. If you're not even kind of confident you want more, you might want to put the brakes on the sex. Because that muddies the waters—for him and for you," Amelia said, her tone careful.

That was the problem. For weeks, I'd been telling myself I didn't know what I wanted when it came to Ward and me. Yet, it was becoming painfully apparent I did know what I wanted. Or rather, what I didn't want. When it came to the idea of cutting off what we shared, my reaction to that was visceral. I couldn't even imagine putting a stop to it. I had no idea, none whatsoever, what to do about it.

Whatever expression crossed my face, Amelia shifted in her chair, sliding her arm around my shoulders and pulling me in for a side hug. "Okay, so it's like that."

Taking a shuddering breath and swallowing through the thickness in my throat, I managed to nod as she leaned back. "I didn't plan any of this. I'm kind of a mess."

Amelia pushed back in her chair, hurrying to the bathroom and returning quickly to slide a box of tissues on the table. It was only then that I felt the hot tear rolling down my cheek.

Snagging a tissue, I glanced amongst my friends. "No one told me what an emotional mess I'd be either. I mean, my doctor said I would experience hormonal swings, but oh my God."

Maisie smiled softly, rolling her eyes. "Oh yeah, I was all over the place." She sobered. "Look, maybe you shouldn't worry so much about sorting everything out now. Maybe it's okay to just play it by ear with Ward."

I shook my head firmly. "No, it's not okay. Some sort of wishy-washy friends with benefits thing is not a good plan. Not when we're having a baby."

Lucy reached across the table, squeezing my hand and handing me another tissue while she was at it. Seeing as I'd nearly shredded the one in my hand, that was a good thing.

"Back to square one. You have to figure out what you want. But we're here no matter what, and if he's an asshole, we'll kick his ass for you," Lucy said.

Scanning the table, a little bubble of joy rose inside. I had awesome friends, and they could actually kick Ward's ass if needed. Maybe not independently, but certainly as a unit.

Driving home later that night, I wondered if Ward was at his place or mine. He'd been staying at mine so often, we didn't really talk about it anymore. I told him I was meeting friends tonight, but that was it.

When I rolled to a stop at the end of my driveway, I was relieved to see his truck there. Because no matter how hard I tried to tell myself it was nothing more than me being sex crazed and pregnant, somewhere in the corners of my heart, I knew I'd miss him if he weren't here.

Walking inside, I found Ward stretched out on the couch, sound asleep. I took the moment to simply look at him. Even in sleep, he was just so damn handsome. His chiseled features were stark in the shadowed light and his dark curls tousled. My eyes traveled down over his body. Even relaxed, every inch of him was sculpted. His T-shirt and jeans did little to mask the raw strength he exuded.

As if he felt me looking at him, his eyes opened—that silvery, smoky gaze locking with mine. My belly flipped, flutters spinning wildly.

On a burst of courage, I sank my hips onto the coffee table, clasping my hands together and finally asking the question I should've asked weeks ago. It was bad enough I didn't know what I wanted, but I didn't even know what he wanted. "What do you want?"

He arched a brow. "I'm not sure what you mean."

"With us?"

The moment felt heavy and uncertain. As he stared at me in the soft light cast from a lamp in the corner, he didn't reply. Not at first. After what felt like forever, but was probably only a few minutes, he reached over, his hand sliding over my knee and down my calf. I hadn't even noticed I was nervously wiggling my foot.

"You," he finally said.

One simple word—so clear, so confident, and so possessive.

Emotion thickened in my throat, and I swallowed, trying to beat back the sense of panic rising inside.

I said nothing. Emotions pummeled me—relief, confusion, frustration. Part of me savored how alpha he was—stating so clearly what he wanted. That same part of me thrilled to the idea it was *me* he wanted. Yet, I was simultaneously annoyed at how susceptible I was to this. Uncertain how to corral the jumble of emotions inside, I didn't reply and turned to look out the window behind me, my courage deflated. The sun had fallen below the horizon, leaving streaks of fading pink in its wake.

All of a sudden, I needed to throw up. Dashing to the bathroom, I was almost annoyed when Ward followed me, brushing my hair back from my face as I vomited into the toilet.

Somehow, it only made it worse that he was so solicitous. Because that was part of what snagged on the corners of my heart and wouldn't let go.

Chapter Thirty-Three
WARD

I nudged the door open with my shoulder, pushing through into the front reception area at the station. With a cup of coffee in one hand and a stack of paperwork in the other, I approached the reception desk. As usual, Maisie was busy, typing away on her computer and responding to a call, something to do with a cat and an excavator.

Maisie glanced up, and I arched a brow because I couldn't help but wonder who the hell she was talking to. She almost started laughing, but she narrowed her eyes and glared at me instead. I turned away, leaning my hips against her desk and taking a long sip of coffee.

Willow Brook Fire & Rescue was on Main Street, close to the center of town. The town was getting busier by the day right now. I hadn't actually visited Willow Brook during my stint up here on firefighting duty a few years back. Yet, I'd heard it was one of many towns in Alaska whose population exploded in the summer. We were well into spring at this point and the tourists kept pouring into town. At the moment, Main Street was bustling with people walking amongst the cutesy shops and restaurants. The variety of tourists was wide—some came simply to enjoy the view and shop, others came for light outdoor activities, while others were hard core and used the location as a launching pad for points all across Alaska for hiking, biking, camping, hunting, fishing and more.

I heard Maisie end her call and turned around. "A cat?" I asked.

She rolled her eyes, removing her headset and setting it on the desk beside her keyboard. "Yes, a cat. That was Carrie Dodge. We're trying to train her to stop using her excavator to get her cat Herman out of trees."

"Huh?"

Maisie smiled wryly. "Yeah, she has her own excavator and she got stuck in it once when it fell in a ditch. If you haven't been out there yet, you will. Herman likes getting stuck in trees. I already called Beck, and he promised me he'd swing by. He'll deal with it."

I couldn't help but chuckle. I loved the fact that Willow Brook was small enough to feel like family. While I had grown up in a small town in Montana, it had expanded by leaps and bounds until it no longer felt small. It was nice to be somewhere like that again.

The next thought dancing along the edges of my mind was that I might just want to stay here beyond my two year commitment. It had occurred to me many, many times that with Susannah's family here, it was highly likely our child would be raised here.

Before I could shy away from that train of thought, my heart gave that odd tumble that happened whenever I thought about Susannah. My mind spun back to the other night when she asked what I thought about us. I knew exactly what I wanted and said as much. She'd pulled back and gone quiet again. My frustration was mounting. I'd been on the verge of demanding she stop denying what was so clear—the connection between us was too powerful to ignore. But she'd gotten sick again, putting a quick end to our conversation, or lack thereof.

Taking a fortifying gulp of my coffee, I handed over the order paperwork Maisie had shown me how to fill out. Holding it in hand, she flipped through the pages, quickly scanning it. She looked up with a grin. "Perfect!"

"Hey, I know how to follow orders."

She grinned again. For a beat, she held my gaze, and I sensed she was considering something. "So I hear you're going to be a father," she said, promptly shocking the hell out of me.

Susannah was starting to show, and I knew she was close friends with Maisie. It only stood to reason her friends would know. I managed a nod and then took another sip of coffee, masking the need to reply right away.

Maisie didn't let me off the hook though. "Just so you know, you'd better treat Susannah right. She's awesome. I know this was a surprise for both of you, but things get serious fast when there's a baby involved."

Despite the urge to run, I forced myself to face her. Because she had a point, a very good one. The awkward part was I was crystal clear about what I wanted. I was fully committed to Susannah and our baby. Yet, I had no clarity on where Susannah stood. Here I had her friend confronting me when she had nothing to worry about. Throwing caution to the wind, I figured I'd lay it on the line.

"Look, I'll be straight with you. I love Susannah, and I'm not going anywhere. I might have been surprised about the baby, but I can roll with it. Problem is, I'm not so sure what Susannah wants."

Maisie stared at me, her mouth dropping open. After a beat, she snapped it shut and cocked her head to one side. "Damn. Well then. I wasn't giving you enough credit."

"It's not like you've known me long. Any suggestions on how to get Susannah to believe this is more than...?" My words trailed off. I might be blunt, but I had some respect. I wasn't about to go into how hot things were between the sheets.

Maisie smiled slowly, a gleam in her eyes. "Right. I get your point. How do you get her to believe this is more than sex? Tell her how you feel."

"I did," I replied quickly.

"You told her you loved her?"

"Well, not exactly that."

Maisie rolled her eyes. "I might not have known you long, but I get the sense you're used to getting what you want. You can't just claim she's yours and make it so. You're gonna have to talk about your *feelings*."

My heart gave a flip. I didn't want to admit it, but she'd zeroed in on it. I was used to getting what I wanted. This might be the first time in my life I wanted a woman the way I wanted Susannah. Certainly, the first time I'd wanted a family. But there was absolutely no question in my mind and heart what I wanted. Yet, I was more about staking my claim, not chatting about my feelings.

I threw a sheepish grin Maisie's way. "Point taken."

"Something else you'd better consider. You need a plan for how you're going to explain it to the crew. As far as I'm concerned, that's more your responsibility than hers," she said pointedly.

"Damn. You're not letting me off easy."

Maisie shrugged. "Nope. It is what it is."

I knew she was right. I took a breath, leaning my elbow on the counter to the side of her desk. "I know, but I keep thinking I need to follow her lead on that."

I couldn't believe I was about to ask Maisie for advice, but I was that desperate. "Any suggestions?"

Her wide brown eyes held mine for a long beat before she nodded slowly. "Sure. Tell her how you feel and respect her wishes," she said flatly. "She's just as surprised as you are by all of this, so keep that in mind."

It occurred to me that Maisie might be able to give me a

few suggestions about Susannah's pregnancy. Every time I tried to ask her questions, she brushed me off. I knew she was having bouts of sickness more than I'd like to see. Strangely, it didn't have the slightest effect on our sex life. We couldn't seem to be in the same bed together without that happening.

"Mind if I ask you a question?"

"Go for it," Maisie said.

"Did you have morning sickness?"

Her brown curls bounced when she nodded. "Is it bad for her?"

Rubbing a hand through my hair, I sighed. "I don't have anything to compare it to. That's why I'm asking you. Seems to happen every other day or so, and I don't know why it's called morning because it happens in the afternoon too."

Maisie smiled softly. "I've only been pregnant once and my doctor—who by the way is the same doctor Susannah has—said it varies for everyone. She also said it usually gets better after the first trimester."

"If my math is right, she's almost through that."

At that moment, the door to the front of the reception area opened and Susannah walked through. I couldn't help it, the moment I saw her, my body tightened. She was so damn beautiful. Her strawberry blonde hair was loose today, her curls falling in a messy tousle around her shoulders and face. Her checks were flushed from the cool spring air. When she looked up and saw me standing beside Maisie, she looked slightly confused, but flashed a quick smile.

As she unzipped her windbreaker, my eyes flicked down to her belly. She was definitely starting to show. Not a lot, but enough that anyone who knew her well would notice.

"Hey there," she said casually as she approached us, leaning her elbows on the counter to the side of Maisie's desk beside me.

Maisie grinned. "Hey, what's up?"

Susannah sighed with a slight roll of her eyes. "I'm

helping Rex today. Apparently, he's got a bunch of stuff for me to work on in the computer files."

Maisie threw her a rueful smile. "Sorry. He's having you help on a project that's been taking me forever because I never have time. He wants to transition all of the old files for the police station into an electronic record. It's pretty tedious. Plus, the station's been around since the 1940's. That's a lot of records. I'd have thought it would've been more boring around here back then."

Susannah laughed softly. "No, this place was close to lawless back then. There was always something happening."

Maisie's gaze coasted over her. "How are you feeling? Ward mentioned you've been having some morning sickness."

The moment Maisie spoke, I realized my mistake. Susannah's eyes bounced from Maisie to me, anger flashing. "I'm fine," she said stiffly.

Unperturbed, Maisie shrugged. "Well, just checking in. Make sure to let Dr. Jenkins know anything unusual."

I was beyond relieved when a call came through for Maisie, conveniently interrupting our conversation. Maisie took the call, waving at us as I turned to go down the back hallway. I held the door open, looking to Susannah. "Wanna come back to my office for a few?"

Whether she wanted to or not, she followed me. I closed the door behind us when she stepped through. Gesturing for her to take a seat at the small round table in the corner, I followed, slipping into a chair across from her.

Susannah wasted no time. "Why the hell are you talking to Maisie about me?"

I lifted my hands up in surrender. "I didn't mean to piss you off. She just asked how you were doing, that's all. Because I'm a man, and apparently an idiot to boot, I've been concerned about how you've been doing, so I asked her about it."

Susannah seemed off—wound tight and tense. She stared

at me for a few moments and then shook her head before looking away.

"Ward," she finally said as she looked back towards me, "I think we need to put the brakes on this right now. Obviously, I know you're going to be a part of my life because we're having a baby. But I'm not sure I'm ready for more. I can't think straight when we keep having sex, so it seems best if we stop seeing each other like that."

My gut started to churn, panic rising in my throat.

Shaking the tension off, I focused on her. "No. I told you what I want. *You*. Maybe you're not ready to hear it, but I love you. It's not just sex, and you damn well know it. Don't you dare shut me out. "

Her eyes narrowed, her lips tightening in a line. She shook her head sharply. "You can't tell me what to do. It's bad enough that you're technically my boss, that I got pregnant, and I have to figure out how to tell the rest of the crew about it. I can't be pushed into this."

She stood abruptly, almost knocking her chair over. There was a rushing sound in my head, my throat tightened with emotion and my heart hammered against my ribs.

"You don't get to call the shots. Right now, we're glorified friends with benefits with a lot more complications than most friends. I'm a big girl, I'll figure it out. But not if you're in my bed every night." She stood abruptly. "I have to go. Please don't come out to my place tonight."

At that, she left quickly, the sound of her cowboy boots striking against the floor down the hallway, marking her departure.

Stunned, I sat there. I was still sitting there when Maisie poked her head through the doorway. "What the hell did you say to her?" she asked, her eyes snapping.

Looking up at Maisie, I threw a glare her way. "Hey, don't blame me. I followed your advice. I told her I loved her, and she walked away."

Maisie's eyes widened. "Oh no."

Chapter Thirty-Four
SUSANNAH

"Mwah!" Maisie exclaimed as she dropped an exaggerated kiss on Max's belly.

I watched as she spun him around on her lap, adjusting the fresh diaper she'd just put on him before she pulled on a lightweight fleece sleeper. Little Max was almost three months old now, a chubby little baby boy with curly dark hair just like his mother's.

My heart squeezed, a wave of emotion hitting me so hard I almost burst into tears. I had started to feel our baby. I'd felt it since I'd known I was pregnant, but now I was having entire conversations with it. I'd somehow convinced myself we were having a little boy. I had many weeks to go before I would know that for certain.

Maisie stood, settling Max in his rocker nearby. Inside of a matter of seconds, he fell asleep. Maisie tucked a blanket over him and then returned, sitting down at the table across from me. We were at her house, the one she shared with Beck. I'd been here many times before, long before I knew Maisie. She'd inherited this house from her grandmother who passed away and left it to her. It had been nicely updated with the living room open and airy and windows floor to ceiling looking out over a field.

Maisie cocked her head to the side. "Are you okay?"

I nodded as I knuckled a random tear away from my cheek. "I've never cried so much in my life," I managed with a sniffle and a soft laugh.

"I know. I was all over the place the whole time I was pregnant. I'm just now starting to feel more normal. Well, except for the fact that I obsess about Max all the time. It's insane to me that before you have a baby, you have a normal life. After you have a baby, they become the center of your entire world. I'd do anything for him. I worry about him all the time, and I feel like it's just a crazy joke. I try to pretend like I'm halfway normal, but it's a challenge."

I swallowed and took a shuddering breath. "Right. Here's hoping I can do this halfway as well as you because you don't seem crazy."

She flashed a grin. "Okay, so far, so good at faking it until I make it. If you don't mind me asking, what happened yesterday with Ward?"

"I told him we needed to stop doing what we've been doing. I can't even say I broke up with him because it's not like we were ever officially together. We were some sort of glorified friends-slash-boss with benefits. We've only been thrown together because I got pregnant." I gave my head a hard shake. "I need to be rational, and I can't think straight when he's over there all the time. Plus, I can't seem to keep my hands off of him," I said bluntly.

Maisie burst out laughing. "Okay. Fair enough." She paused, sobering. "He told me he loved you," she said carefully. "For what it's worth, he looked really upset after you left."

Hope tried to wave a flag inside, but I ignored it. "I just feel boxed in, like how do I know what I really want? I feel bad enough that I threw this whole thing on him. I'm trying to deal with it as best I can, but we have to be adults. As it is, I'm not sure what to tell the crew. It's one thing to tell them I'm pregnant, but it's another thing to tell them our new boss is the father. It's going to be a mess."

Maisie was quiet for a beat, glancing away briefly when Max made a gurgling sound in his sleep. Looking back to me, she shrugged. "I don't think it's gonna be that big of a deal. It's not like others don't get involved with each other. I guess it might be a thing that he's your new boss, but you guys knew each other before and had that relationship before."

"Relationship?"

"Oh, you know what I mean. It's not like this was the first time you had sex with him."

"Yeah, and because I'm amazing, I managed to get pregnant only the second time we had sex," I said with a roll of my eyes.

Maisie chuckled, shaking her head slowly. Sobering again, she eyed me. "Look, I don't know him that well, but I think he really loves you. You should see the way he looks when he talks about you. I'm worried you're letting great sex get in the way." She paused and rolled her eyes. "Okay, that sounded weird, but I think you get my point."

"I'm letting sex get in the way? Oh my God. Look, you and Beck…"

Now Maisie got annoyed. "Don't even go there. Relationships aren't simple. Just because Beck and I figured things out didn't mean it was easy. Stop throwing up roadblocks."

It was too much. Even though part of me knew I needed to listen, I was tired. And lonely. Nights without Ward sucked. I started crying again. Which was ridiculous. I wasn't much of a crier, but lately I was like a leaky faucet. "Can we talk about something else?" I managed between breaths.

Her warm brown eyes held mine. "Oh hon, I get it. Okay, what can I do to help?"

"You're already doing it," I said simply.

Because she was that kind of friend, Maisie nodded and

started filling me in on the latest harmless gossip. As the primary dispatcher for Willow Brook Fire & Rescue, she was one of the nerve centers in town.

Not much later, I was on my way out. Standing at the door as I started to walk away, she said my name. "Zanna?"

Glancing back, I asked, "Yes?"

"I respect how you feel, but don't shut Ward out. I have a feeling about you two."

Turning back, I gave her a quick hug before jogging to my car. I couldn't manage to speak because I wanted to cry again.

Chapter Thirty-Five
WARD

A full week had passed since Susannah basically told me to fuck off. Actually, that wasn't quite fair. She had her reasons for asking me to back off, but I was still pissed at the world for it.

As for how I felt? Devastated.

I missed her so much it hurt. And it had only been a week. I marveled at how quickly I'd gotten comfortable with her. I worried about her and our baby all the time. I kept coming up with excuses to stop by or to call her, but every time I talked myself out of it.

Giving my head a shake, I turned my truck into the parking lot behind Wildlands Lodge. I was meeting a couple of the guys here. I supposed it was good that I wasn't spending every night at Susannah's now. I hadn't made much of an effort to socialize with the crew. As one of the newer members of the crew, they needed to be comfortable with me, more so because I was in charge. Beck and Cade had all but ordered me here this evening.

Walking in, I glanced around, my eyes landing on them in the corner. Threading my way through the tables, I noticed Chad at the bar and experienced a twinge of anger from my last encounter with him. Although I couldn't get Susannah out of my thoughts, Chad was easy. The moment he was out of sight, I forgot about him.

Joining Cade and Beck at the table, I settled in with a beer and chatted with them and the other guys as they began to trickle in from the station. We'd had a fairly busy week at work and had even flown out briefly to assist with a controlled burn in an area with a high percentage of dead trees. For the first time in my life, I loved my job not just because I enjoyed it, but because it kept me busy. Busy was good. Busy kept my thoughts off of Susannah, mostly.

In a lull in the conversation, Beck leaned over. "So how's Susannah?"

"I wouldn't know," I replied, shifting my shoulders and taking a drag on my beer.

"Ah. So that's how it is? Maisie mentioned something to me about it, but she's all protective of Susannah, so I wasn't sure how accurate it was. You two break up?"

I spun my almost empty beer bottle between my fingers and shrugged. "Not sure I could say we were ever officially together."

"You were together enough to get her pregnant and then some," Beck said flatly.

I sensed he was trying to tell me what the hell to do and offer support at the same time. "Look, I don't need you to be on my side. There is no side here. I put my cards on the table, and she asked me to back the hell off. I'm trying to give her a little space before I storm my way back in."

Beck leaned his elbows on the table, his eyes widening in disbelief. "That's cool with you?"

"Didn't you and Cade tell me Susannah doesn't like to be told what to do?"

"Well yeah, but things change. I saw her at the station the other day, and she looks miserable. Now might be the time to push things along. Unless you want to be a bystander in her life and your baby's life," he said pointedly.

Damn. Beck's usual easygoing manner masked how blunt he could be. My internal reaction was so strong I almost slammed my fist on the table. Because if I had my way? Hell no.

Whatever Beck saw in my eyes, he nodded slowly. "That's what I thought. Don't let this slide. Not now. You'll get nothing if you don't try. You don't even have a shot without trying. It's like turning your back and walking away. You don't strike me as a quitter."

Chapter Thirty-Six
WARD

A few beers later, I saw Susannah walk into the restaurant with Maisie, Amelia, and Lucy. The moment I saw her, my entire body tightened. Pure longing pierced through me. Fuck. I missed her like crazy.

Beck and Levi were over in the corner playing a game of pool. Meanwhile, Cade was still at the table with me and a few other guys from the station. Lucy and Maisie broke in the direction of Beck and Levi, while Amelia headed our way. Susannah didn't appear to have seen me and approached the bar.

I watched as she paused and said hello to a woman I didn't recognize. I'd forgotten Chad was here and saw his eyes travel over to her. Oh, hell no. I forced myself to hold still for a moment, as if to give him a chance not to piss me off.

No such luck. He pushed away from the bar at the far corner and approached Susannah directly. Whatever he said, I could see her face tighten from where I was.

Shoving my chair back, I stood, threading my way

through the crowd. The moment I reached Susannah's side, her eyes flicked to mine, her expression carefully controlled.

"Hey," I said simply.

For a beat, I thought she wasn't going to reply, but then she did. "Hey, how's it going?" At my nod, she gestured to the woman at her side. "Ward, this is Levi's mother, Gloria Phillips."

Her comment threw me. I was attuned to Chad's presence, not polite conversation. Forcing myself to focus, I looked to the woman beside Susannah. "Nice to meet you. Levi's a great guy," I managed.

Gloria grinned, Levi's resemblance to her obvious with her golden hair and blue eyes just like his. With a wink, she replied, "Of course he is. I'm his mother, so I wouldn't have allowed anything else. Welcome to Willow Brook, although I understand you've been here over a month. What do you think so far?"

"It's good to be here, and I'm glad to be at the station. Great team to work with," I replied.

Gloria smiled and nodded, glancing away when someone else called her name. Turning back, she reached over to squeeze Susannah's shoulder. "Good to see you dear. Let me know if you need anything, okay?"

"Of course, same to you," Susannah said.

Gloria's eyes caught mine again with another smile. "Very nice to meet you, Ward. I hope to be seeing much more of you."

Her words seemed weighted, containing a meaning I didn't quite understand. Yet, then it occurred to me, she was likely friends with Susannah's mother. As such, she may be aware that Susannah was pregnant.

"I'm sure you will. Nice to meet you," was my bland reply.

With those niceties over as Gloria walked away, I glanced back to Susannah. I was well aware that Chad was still nearby and his eyes were on us. Before I had a chance to say anything, he did.

"So what does the crew think of the fact that you guys are fucking?" Chad asked his lip curling in a sneer.

Susannah's face turned white and then bright red, her breath hissing through her teeth. Several of the guys from the crew happened to be nearby and within earshot. I felt a few curious eyes cast our way. I ignored them. Turning to face Chad, anger flashed hot inside. "What the fuck did you just say?" I asked, my tone nearly vibrating.

It didn't matter to me that what he said had been true until a week ago. Hell, I didn't care if he was trying to call me out. But trying to humiliate Susannah publicly like this – not fucking okay.

Chad rolled his eyes, his flat brown gaze flicking between Susannah and me. "You heard what I said. What I can't figure out is how you got this frigid bitch to let you get in her pants."

Everything went red in my brain. I didn't think about where we were, or who happened to be around. I took one step, drawing my fist back and grabbing Chad by the shirt with my other hand. Lifting him off the floor, I drove my fist into his face.

He cried out, blood spurting from his nose as my fist connected. In a flash, I felt someone tugging me away. I tried to shake them off.

"Ward, let go," someone's voice said clearly in my ear.

Spinning back, I saw Cade. He had an iron grip on my arm. I could easily take Chad in a fight. But Cade? Not so easy. We were about even, almost precisely the same height and size. He was strong and muscled, and he meant business. I didn't think he would hesitate to use force to keep me from being any more stupid than I already had.

Still, I tried to shake free from his grip again. The spectacle drew a cluster of people around us. Beck and Levi arrived to drag Chad off the floor and lug him out of the way. Levi made quick work of shooing the bystanders away.

My eyes searched for Susannah and found her standing at the edge of the circle. Her gaze was wide, and she looked pissed. "Zanna…" I started to say.

She shook her head sharply, her gaze swinging to Chad, laser focused. Although Beck had him out of the way, she strode straight to him. Without the slightest hesitation, she drew back and punched him square in the face. "Fuck you, Chad. You're too much of an idiot to realize you're not worth anyone's time."

Damn, she was glorious when she was angry.

At that, she spun away and started walking towards the back.

Forgetting Cade had a grip on my arm, I started to follow her, only to get yanked back promptly. "Where the hell do you think you're going?"

"I need to talk to her," I said. "I know that wasn't a good move but you didn't hear what he said."

"Oh, I did. Can't say I blame you. I'm just trying to keep it from getting any worse than it already is. As it is, if Chad wants to press charges, my dad will go along with it. He follows the rules," Cade said with a roll of his eyes.

"I don't care," I said flatly. "I just need to talk to Susannah."

Whatever Cade saw in my eyes, he finally let go of my arm. For a flash, I saw a hint of empathy in his gaze. My heart tightened. I could imagine I looked frantic. Inside, I was. I needed to get to Susannah. Now. "If your dad shows up, tell him I'll be right back."

At Cade's nod and finally free of his iron grip, I almost ran across the room, catching sight of Susannah just as she turned into the back hallway. I caught up to her quickly. "Susannah!"

She spun back, her eyes fairly snapping. "What the hell, Ward? What was that about?"

"He called you a frigid bitch. I can't just stand there when someone does that."

"I can take care of myself," she retorted.

We stared at each other, the air heavy, crowded with unspoken words and feelings. Every moment near her, my heart pounded so hard, my entire body was vibrating from the force of its beat.

A full week had passed since I'd seen her and the simple sight of her sent emotion cascading through me. My throat was tight, and I could hardly get a breath. She stared at me for a beat and then looked away.

A group of customers came in the back door. Susannah kept her face turned away from mine as they walked by us in the hallway. Glancing around quickly as yet another group of customers came in the back, I waited until they passed us by and then tugged her into the small restroom in the hallway.

She yanked her arm away from me once I shut the door behind us. "What the hell are you doing?" she hissed. "You have no right. Chad's an asshole, he's always been an asshole, and he's always going to be an asshole. Just because he said something shitty doesn't mean you get to hit him and make a scene. And to be clear, I don't really care that you hit him, but I do care about the scene you made."

Her eyes were bright with tears. I stepped to her and tried to reach for her instinctively. She held herself tensely, not quite pushing me away, but certainly not relaxing into me. She wouldn't look at me.

In a flash, I understood the concept of a broken heart. Because right now, with her physically and emotionally shoving me away, my heart felt like it was cracking into two pieces. The pain of it was so intense, I could hardly stand it.

"Zanna..."

She finally looked at me, her gorgeous eyes flashing. "Don't call me that."

"I know you can take care of yourself. It doesn't change the fact I love you."

She stared at me, her eyes widening and then a tear rolling down her cheek. She took a deep breath and then suddenly burst into tears. This time, she didn't hold herself away when I pulled her into my arms.

Chapter Thirty-Seven
SUSANNAH

The fabric of Ward's shirt was damp against my cheek as I took another shuddering breath. I couldn't seem to stop crying. But then, I supposed that made sense. I'd been trying to keep up a brave front all week and not fall apart, but I missed him so much. His absence made everything feel lonely.

There was all of that and then the fact that I'd fallen in love with him. My emotions were so raw, I couldn't talk myself out of my feelings any more. Oh, and I was pregnant. I felt like I was hurtling down a path I hadn't chosen. Yet, I had no choice but to keep going.

He felt so strong and steady as he held me. One hand traced in circles on my back, while the other sifted through my hair where my head rested against his chest. He smelled so good, that woodsy, citrusy scent he carried. I tried to remember if I'd ever noticed how a man smelled before. I couldn't seem to recall. But Ward's scent? I knew I'd never forget it.

I was mortified I'd fallen apart like this. I was also too tired emotionally to stop it. I hadn't slept worth a damn all week. After a few long moments, there was a knock at the door.

"Susannah?" Maisie's muffled voice came through the door.

"Do you want to talk to her?" Ward asked, his tone careful and low.

I shook my head against his chest. "Not right now," I mumbled into his shirt.

"Susannah?" Maisie asked again. "Just let me know you're okay."

"Can I tell her you're okay?"

At my nod against his chest, his hand dropped from my hair, and I felt him turn slightly. His back was to the door, so he had to reach behind himself to open it. The bathroom here was tiny. There was hardly enough room for the two of us in here. We stood between the wall and the sink with only inches on either side.

"She's okay," Ward said through the crack in the door when he opened it.

"Are you sure? I want to talk to her," Maisie said, her tone firm.

Ward didn't seem to take the slightest offense at her insistence. I felt him nodding and then his voice rumbled in his chest. "Hang on."

I looked up now, realizing I could only hide my face in his shirt but for so long. His eyes met mine, the concern there almost making me burst into tears again. "I don't think she's going away until she can talk to you."

"I can hear you, you know," Maisie called from outside the door.

I couldn't help but laugh. I had protective friends. "I'm okay," I called over Ward's shoulder. "I promise."

"That's all I needed to hear," Maisie said and then the door closed again.

Ward reached behind him to lock it and then lifted his

hand to brush my tangled hair away from my face. It was damp from my tears and rubbing my face against his shirt. When I sniffled, he leaned over and snagged some toilet paper from the roll before handing it to me. "It's not tissue, but..."

"It's fine," I said as I took it from him.

Blowing my nose noisily, I dabbed at my cheeks and then tossed the tissue in the wastebasket under the sink. I caught sight of my face in the mirror as I turned back to face him. My checks were splotchy pink and my eyes were red from crying. I looked like hell. Mustering my courage, I looked up at him finally.

His eyes met mine, his gaze steady, but slightly uncertain. That was a new look for him. We stared at each other in the tiny bathroom with the muffled sounds from the bar drifting down the narrow hallway. I heard another cluster of people coming in the back door, their footsteps echoing as they walked into the restaurant.

"I didn't mean to fall apart like that. You could say it's been a long week," I finally said.

He was quiet as his gaze coasted over my face. He brushed my hair back again, tucking a few loose curls behind my ear. As it always did when he was near me, my body betrayed me. Goose bumps ran in a shiver from the side of my neck down to my toes at nothing more than a brush of his fingertips behind my ear.

"It has been a long week." His voice was low and gruff, his eyes intent on mine. "I missed you every day. Every minute. How are you feeling?"

"Well, I'm not getting sick as much, but I want to eat weird things." Gulping in air, I decided to be honest because I'd already made a fool of myself. "I miss you. This is a mess. You don't have to tell me you love me."

His eyes flashed silver, and he cupped my face with both of his hands, his gaze burning into me. "I know I don't have to. But I do."

"Are you...?" I started to ask. My mouth went dry when he shook his head sharply.

"I don't say things I don't mean. I love you. Like I said before."

Staring at him, I was hit with another wave of emotion and before I knew it, tears were rolling hot down my cheeks. I wiped them away with my sleeve. Glancing back up, I found him looking startled and concerned, as if he didn't quite know what to do with me like this.

I didn't quite know what to do with me like this.

"Zanna, I'm sorry. I know it's a lot," he muttered as he leaned over and grabbed more toilet paper, carefully dabbing at my cheeks before handing it to me. I blew my nose again and then took a deep breath.

"It's not you. I love you, and I'm a mess. I mean, look at me," I said, gesturing to my face.

He did as I asked, his mouth hitching at the corner with a smile. "You look beautiful."

Rolling my eyes, I blew my nose once more. "Right. I think you're just being nice now."

With another shake of his head, he pulled me back into his arms. I felt his shoulders rise and fall with a deep breath, his body relaxing slightly as he pulled me closer. It was then that I noticed the feel of his hard cock between us, pressing against my low belly. My channel clenched in response.

As if he could read my mind, he said, "Ignore it. I don't have much control over myself when I'm near you. I promise I didn't drag you into this bathroom for that."

I giggled. "It's all good. We have a mutual problem," I said, leaning my head back with a grin.

We stood there grinning at each other, a sense of giddiness spinning through me. There was another knock at the door. This time, an unfamiliar voice filtered through the thin door. "Gonna be out anytime soon? I kinda need to pee."

I burst out laughing again, Ward right along with me. He called out, "Give us a minute."

When he looked back down at me, his gaze sobered. "If Chad wants to be a jerk, Cade warned me we might get charged."

I'd completely forgotten the events that led to me storming down the hallway. "For what it's worth, please don't go around hitting guys for me. I can take care of myself."

He shrugged, completely unrepentant. "If any guy, Chad or otherwise, talks about you like that, I reserve the right to hit them."

Staring at him, I shook my head. I just had to go and fall in love with a tough, alpha guy. So be it. With another roll of my eyes, I stepped back, not that there was much space for it. "Okay, I suppose we should face the music."

He stood there, looking at me for a beat, lifting his hands to brush my hair back again, his palms cupping my cheeks. "I meant what I said. I love you. If you're wondering what that means, it means you'll never be rid of me."

My heart was pounding so hard, I could hardly breathe. Joy swirled inside. "I love you too. I think we have to save the rest of this for later. Nature calls for someone," I said, just as there was another knock at the door.

Chapter Thirty-Eight
WARD

Much, much later that night, I climbed under the covers beside Susannah. As much as I'd wanted to hurry away from Wildlands earlier, Rex hadn't allowed me. While I'd been in the bathroom with Susannah, someone had made a call to the police. We'd lucked out, if only because after I hauled off and punched Chad and then Susannah hit him, he'd been drunk enough to try to punch Beck and Levi when they dragged him out of the mess the second time.

As luck would have it, he managed to land a punch on Beck's cheek. So Rex gave us a scolding and gave Chad a choice. Either all of us got charged, or none of us got charged. Chad might be an asshole, but he wasn't stupid. He decided he didn't want to face charges, so we were off the hook.

Then, Susannah had asked me to go ahead and talk to the few crewmembers from our crew who happened to be witness to the entire messy debacle. With her permission to gloss over our history, I'd told them we'd been involved before and so on and so forth. Unbeknownst to me, Susannah had also decided during the week we'd been apart that it was a wise move for her to switch over from one of the hotshot crews to the local crew.

As she'd pointed out, "We're having a baby. We can't both be going out in the middle of nowhere at the same time. This way, I'll still be doing what I love, but I'll always be home."

I couldn't say I was one hundred percent on board with that choice, but I knew it was the smart choice. I also knew I needed to let Susannah make her own decisions, so I'd have to accept there would be weeks when we'd be apart. Given the alternative—leaving our baby with someone else—it was definitely the best option.

I was so fucking relieved to be climbing into bed with Susannah. She was resting on her side, so I followed suit, curling up behind her. She was warm and silky, every inch of her feeling like heaven. When the hard ridge of my cock bumped into her bottom, I murmured, "Ignore it."

She giggled and reached between us behind her back, her palm curling over my hard length. "What if I don't feel like it?" she asked, her voice husky.

"I don't think I can say no. Not to you."

Then, I was breathing in the scent of her, tasting her skin with my lips and tongue as I blazed a trail of kisses down her neck and over her shoulder, my hand cupping her breasts and teasing her nipples.

She'd crawled into bed bare ass naked. It would've taken an act of God to keep me from making love to her. When my hand slid down over her belly, her voice caught my attention.

"Can you tell I'm putting on weight?"

I let my palm coast over the subtle curve of her belly. "I wouldn't call it 'weight.' I call it curves. The more, the better, as far as I'm concerned. In fact, you're hot as hell pregnant."

When she giggled, I slipped my fingers through her curls, dipping them into the moisture between her thighs, finding her hot, slick and ready.

I didn't want to wait, it had been too long. A single week had felt like forever. Reaching between us, I lifted one of her legs, resting it over mine, giving me more access to tease her. In a matter of seconds, she was rocking her hips back against me.

"Ward, please."

With need pounding through me, I gripped my cock in my fist, sliding my other hand over the curve of her lush ass. Pushing it apart and making room for me, in one subtle shift, I sank into the warm, clenching heat of her core.

I held still for a beat, savoring how it felt to hold her close against me and be buried deep inside of her. She was home to me. Or rather *we* were home to me.

Brushing her hair away from her cheek, I rested mine against hers as I rocked into her. Her channel throbbed and pulsed around my cock, nearly pushing me over the edge instantly. Skimming a hand down over her breasts and belly again, I teased her wet folds, circling over her clit.

She cried out, my name a husky gasp. Her channel clamped down around me as she found her release, sending my climax thundering through me.

I held her close, absorbing the feel of her. For the first time in weeks, I felt relaxed. I hadn't consciously realized what an effort it had been to keep my feelings caged inside.

After a moment, she spoke. "Well, so much for telling myself I could keep my hands off of you."

"I think that was my fault."

She giggled and started to roll over, but I shook my head. "Don't move."

"How come?" she asked.

"Because I want to stay right here. Forever would work."

I felt her smile against my cheek and her hand lifting up

to ruffle my hair. "I'm going to have to pee in a minute," she said. "It happens all the time now."

I reluctantly drew back, sliding up to rest against the pillows as she slipped out of bed. Within seconds, she returned, slipping under the covers beside me. She curled up against me, her fingers tracing circles on my chest.

"I want to get a dog," she said out of nowhere.

My laugh slipped out unbidden. "Okay, you want to get a dog? Where did this come from?"

"I've always wanted one, but I felt like my job wasn't a good fit. But if we're going to have a baby and I'm switching to one of the local crews, then we can have a dog."

My heart squeezed so hard it hurt. "If you want a dog, we'll get a dog."

Chapter Thirty-Nine
SUSANNAH

Sliding my hips onto the examination table, I shivered slightly at the feel of the cool, crinkly paper under my hips. The thin cotton gown did little to keep me warm in the always chilly room. I glanced over at Ward, swinging my feet restlessly. My heart gave a little kick to my ribs when I saw the look on his face. He was looking at me, his gorgeous silver-smoke gaze steady. The muscle ticking in his jaw gave away a hint of nervousness though.

He swallowed, the sound audible in the small examination room. I was twenty-two weeks along now, and we were here for my scheduled ultrasound. Today, we could find out if it was a boy or a girl. We'd had a funny discussion about it this morning with Ward declaring he didn't want to know if it was a girl because, if it was, he'd probably have a heart attack.

Hands on hips, I'd glared at him. "What's wrong with a girl?"

He'd spun to face me where he stood by the counter. "Nothing, absolutely nothing. I'm just afraid I'll worry a lot more."

"Have you ever worried about me?" I'd countered.

In two long strides, he was standing right in front of me. His hands lifted to cup my cheeks. "Yes. The whole time we were in training together, I worried about you. Not because I didn't think you could handle yourself. It was never that. You're stronger, smarter, and braver than probably any man I know. Hell, most women probably are. It's just you mean too much. It's all I can do to deal with worrying about you."

My heart kicked up a notch at his words. I lost my words entirely. For a man who didn't talk very often, when he did, he took my breath away.

As I recalled that conversation, his eyes broke from mine to study the floor in the examination room. Within seconds, he glanced back up as if he sensed my gaze on him. I smiled. "Don't worry so much. It'll be fine."

He shook his head, a bark of a laugh coming out. Leaning back, he shifted his shoulders with a sigh. "Doctors make me nervous."

At that moment, there was a quick knock on the door. Ward looked at me, his brow furrowing in confusion.

"They always knock just to make sure it's okay to come in," I explained. "Come in," I called out.

Dr. Jenkins stepped into the room, closing the door behind her and adjusting her glasses. Her gaze bounced between us. "How are we today?" she asked

"Better. Like you said, the queasiness is wearing off. It's not as bad as it was for a few weeks there."

Nodding, she adjusted her lab coat as she slipped onto the stool nearby, spinning the attached monitor toward her. Clicking a few keys on the keyboard, she scanned the screen and then turned to me. "So have you decided?"

I glanced to Ward.

"Why are you looking at me?" he asked.

"Well, we weren't sure this morning."

A smile teased at the corners of his mouth, and he lifted

a shoulder in an easy shrug. "Let's find out. That way we can get used to the idea."

Dr. Jenkins' lips quirked, but she stayed quiet. Ward caught her eye with a sheepish smile. "Go ahead and laugh. I don't know what the hell I'm doing. I've never had a baby. I mean, I've never been about to be a father," he clarified.

She did laugh then. "There's a first time for everything. No matter what, it'll be an adventure. Plus, you're here"—she paused, her gaze sobering—"and that says a lot."

Ward simply nodded, leaning forward in his chair and resting his elbows on his knees.

She stood, glancing to me then. "Okay, you know the drill."

Rolling onto my back on the table, the sound of the paper crinkling was distinctly loud. In short order, she was handing me the wand and asking me to guide it inside. She squirted the gel for the ultrasound on my belly, and I was pleasantly surprised to discover it was warm. "Oh that's nice. I was bracing myself."

She flashed a quick smile. "I know. We got a heater. Believe it or not, we had to get special permission for that."

Ward was quiet from where he sat. I felt her sliding the rolled instrument over my belly, and she adjusted the wand inside of me. Within a few moments, she was speaking softly.

"Everything looks great. Can you see?"

I craned my neck to see the screen, the grainy black and white view coming into focus. "See, there's the head," she said, gesturing to the screen.

I felt Ward stand, coming to the side of the table, one of his hands resting on my calf, his touch warm. I was overcome with emotion—to have him here, to have this happening. Even though it was all a big accident, sometimes accidents were the best thing ever.

"Okay, last chance to tell me you don't want to know if it's a boy or a girl," Dr. Jenkins said softly.

Rolling my head, I glanced over to Ward. His eyes caught mine. For a beat, it was as if we were all alone. Intimacy arced between us, alive and shimmering in the cool air, both of us asking each other the same question without saying a word.

At his gentle nod, I answered, "We want to know."

"It's a boy."

Wild joy spun inside my heart. Ward held my gaze, a smile tugging at the corners of his mouth.

"Well, I guess you don't have to worry then, do you?"

He gave my calf another squeeze, his hand sliding up over my knee. "Oh no, there's still plenty to worry about."

Staring at him, I was suddenly overwhelmed with emotion. Again. I was smiling so hard, my face hurt. I didn't realize I was crying until Dr. Jenkins handed me a tissue.

"I'll give you two a few minutes alone," she said before quickly helping me remove the wand and wiping the gel off my belly.

Flashing a warm smile between us, she stepped out. "I'll be back in a few. There are a few more things we have to go over."

As soon as the door clicked shut behind her, Ward leaned over, startling me when he caught my lips in a kiss. As he drew back, he brushed my hair off my cheek, the tenderness in his gaze nearly making me cry all over again.

"I really don't care if it's a boy or a girl. I'm just glad it's you and me and whatever is about to happen next," he murmured.

I stared at him, my heart thudding hard and fast. I couldn't quite believe this man—who I'd thought would be nothing more than one night and a searing memory, burned into my heart and soul—was now a permanent part of my life.

A few days later, I was in the kitchen at Ward's house. Somehow over the last few weeks, we'd migrated over to his place more frequently. Perhaps because he had more space. Although I loved my little cabin, it hadn't been built with a family in mind.

Opening one of the cabinets, I pulled out a cutting board and started chopping vegetables.

I discovered Ward loved when I cooked. I happened to be fairly good at it, so I'd been making an effort to have dinner ready for him whenever he got home. With my new, mostly normal schedule now, it worked for me to do it. Plus, I enjoyed seeing the surprise on his face every night.

Hearing the sound of tires coming down the driveway, I couldn't help the tightening in my belly and the butterflies amassing there. I doubted I would ever lose the sense of anticipation I felt when it came to him. I stayed busy chopping vegetables, forcing myself not to run to the window and stare outside like a foolish girl with a crush.

As it was, he surprised me. I heard him step inside and the door close behind him. All of a sudden, there was a scurrying sound across the floor and something was twining around my feet. I glanced down to see a small bundle of brown fur wiggling like mad against my legs. "Oh my God! It's a puppy."

I leaned over and lifted it up into my arms. A quick glance and I knew it was a girl. She had curly, silky brown fur, and honestly, she looked like a little brown mop. Her wide brown eyes were barely visible amongst the fur. I snuggled her against my shoulder, laughing when she started licking my face.

Glancing over, I saw Ward as he leaned his hand against the counter, watching me with the puppy. "Jesse's dog had puppies two months ago, so I thought I'd surprise you. She was the only one left."

I looked at the puppy again and almost burst into tears. I'd cried more in the last few months then I'd ever cried in my life, although I cried as much with joy as anything the last few weeks. Ward, somber and serious by nature with such a tendency to keep to himself, continued to surprise me with how sweet he could be.

Ward was at my side in a flash. "Why are you crying?"

I grinned as a tear rolled down my cheek. "I'm happy. I can't believe you did this."

He stared at me, his eyes flashing silver. "I'd do anything for you."

EPILOGUE

Ward

Looking out the window of the small plane, I watched the mountains pass by underneath us. The sky was clear today and the sun high, casting its rays over the snowcapped peaks. The ocean was visible in the distance, telling me we were close to Willow Brook.

For me, Willow Brook was home now. I loved the little town, but that wasn't why it felt like home. It was home because Susannah and Wayne were there. They were my life, the sun in my universe now.

I'd been gone for three weeks, three weeks too long. I still loved my job. Yet, whenever we had to fly out to the backcountry to deal with a fire, I missed them the whole time. On the heels of a deep breath, I leaned my head back against the seat, rolling it to the side to see Beck checking his phone. He glanced up, catching my eyes.

"Lemme guess," I said. "Checking in with Maisie?"

He flashed a grin. "Of course. You know what it's like now. You've got a family waiting for you."

I had no trouble admitting I'd do anything for them. I

returned Beck's grin. "I sure do know. Being away is the only thing I don't like about our job."

Beck nodded. "Completely agree. But it keeps everything in perspective."

Later that night, or more specifically in the middle of the night, I rested against the pillows while Susannah nursed Wayne. A lamp in the far corner of the bedroom caught the soft gold in her hair. I looked over at her, thinking I'd never ever get tired of the sight of her.

Her strawberry curls fell in a tousle around her shoulders, and her eyes looked tired. She was so damn beautiful. I ran a fingertip down the side of her neck and over the curve of her shoulder. Her gaze caught mine, her mouth hitching at the corner in a sleepy smile. "I keep hoping he'll sleep through the night."

"Well, he's only waking up once a night now. He's hungry. At least he goes right back to sleep after you nurse him."

She nodded, glancing down at his dark curls and sifting her fingers through them. We fell into quiet while she nursed him, and I rested beside her. The silence was comfortable. But then, I was always comfortable with her.

After a few minutes, Wayne fell asleep, his mouth finally releasing her nipple. She stood carefully and stepped into the small room off to the side where his crib was. Within minutes, she returned to bed. I figured whoever designed this house must've had a baby in mind because that little room right off the main bedroom was perfect for a baby.

Sliding back under the covers, she looked over to me as she curled against my side. "You know, you don't have to wake up every night with me. You need your sleep."

Shrugging, I shook my head. "I want to. I hate that I have to miss a few weeks every so often. So when I'm here, it's a team effort. I'd nurse him if I could, but he likes you better."

Susannah smiled softly. "Okay, I just didn't want you to think I expected it."

Because I was that bad when it came to her, I lifted a hand, trailing it down the silky skin of her neck to trace around one of her nipples. Major bonus, her already lush curves were even more full now. I fucking loved every inch of her.

When her breath hissed, I glanced up, catching her eyes as they darkened. I thanked God for the thousandth time—at least I wasn't alone in how much I felt for her. Reaching for her, I tugged her into my lap, groaning at the feel of her slick folds over my cock.

"Wow, you're ready," she observed with a giggle.

"It's been three weeks too long." Staring at her, my heart clenched tightly reminding me, yet again, I would do anything for her.

"Did I forget to tell you I loved you today?"

She shook her head, a grin teasing at the corners of her mouth.

"Oh good," I murmured as I tugged her down to me, catching her lips in a kiss.

Thank you for reading Hot Mess - I hope you loved Susannah & Ward's story!

For more smoking hot firefighter romance, Caleb & Ella's story is up next in Burn So Good. Caleb & Ella were high school sweethearts torn apart by tragedy. Their second chance romance is epic. "Fun, enjoyable, heartwrenching, intense, and at times hard to put down! Thrilling hot chemistry!" Don't miss Caleb's story!

Keep reading for a sneak peek!

Be sure to sign up for my newsletter for the latest news, teasers & more! Click here to sign up: http://jhcroixauthor.com/subscribe/

EXCERPT: BURN SO GOOD BY J.H. CROIX; ALL RIGHTS RESERVED

CALEB

The chilly rain pelted against my face as I leapt out of the truck. Dashing across the highway, I hurried around the car lying on its side in the ditch. The driver's side was crumpled, and I couldn't get a good look at the driver. "Hello? Say something if you can hear me," I called.

Nothing but the sound of the rain drumming on the car answered me.

With my heart pounding out a staccato beat, I scanned the scene. The ground was muddy and slick. If I was going to have any luck checking on the driver and getting whoever it was out, I'd have to climb on top of the vehicle, which happened to be the passenger side at the moment. Oblivious to the rain, I rounded the wrecked car and pulled myself up. The passenger side window was broken, so I carefully knocked the glass loose to the ground and glanced through.

"Hey..."

My words clogged up in my throat, and my heart took off like a rocket. Ella Masters was in a crumpled ball, mostly toward the dashboard. A trickle of blood ran down her cheek. I had to force myself to stay focused. This went from a routine rescue to something far too personal the second I laid eyes on her.

"Ella, Ella!"

I tried to keep my voice calm, but I could feel the sense of panic rising inside. When she didn't reply, I almost did something stupid and started to crawl through the window. A jagged edge of torn metal caught the sleeve of my jacket, nudging me enough to shake free of the panic.

Pausing, I took stock. Reaching through the window, I rested two fingertips against Ella's wrist where it lay limply on the steering wheel. I breathed a sigh of relief when I felt her pulse. The nightmarish feeling inside subsided marginally. I still needed to get her out, but at least I knew she was alive.

Fumbling in my pocket, I yanked my cellphone out, quickly making a call.

"Nine-one-one, what's your emergency?"

"Hey Maisie, it's Caleb. Accident out on the highway."

"Already paging the crew on duty. I'm confirming your location now," Maisie replied swiftly. "Anything I need to tell them?"

"Just that it's Ella Masters. You might want to give Cade a heads up if he's headed this way," I said, referring to Ella's older brother who happened to work with me at Willow Brook Fire & Rescue.

"Is she okay?" Maisie asked calmly.

Looking over at Ella's face, my heart clenched and panic gripped my chest like a vise. Pushing back against it, I swallowed. "She's got a pulse, but she's unconscious." Scanning over her, I absorbed the details. She had a bleeding gash on her forehead and her body was tucked up toward the roof. By some miracle, I didn't see any other injuries, although I couldn't see too much. Rain was falling through the broken window. Her face was damp and her skin was turning bluish.

"You have my location?" I asked Maisie, the ever-reliable dispatcher for our station.

"Of course. Crew's about three minutes away. It's Beck's team. I'll give Cade a call to let him know," she said softly.

"Okay. I'm gonna go. I think I can get her out of the vehicle. Bye."

"Be..."

I assumed she meant to tell me to be careful, but I didn't wait to hear it. Stuffing my phone back in my pocket, I took a steadying breath and then carefully stepped back. With my feet on the back door, I managed to open the other door. Moving carefully, I wedged my hips against the door to hold it open and reached in for Ella.

The moment I curled my hands around both of hers, I nearly lost my balance when she spoke. "Caleb?"

My eyes whipped to her face. Her wide green eyes met mine, hazy and confused. "What happened? Why are you here?"

I was so damn relieved she was conscious, emotion tightened in my chest. "You had an accident. I was driving back from Anchorage and stopped to check. An emergency team is on the way, but I'm trying to see if we can get you out of here first. How do you feel?"

Ella stared at me, and it felt as if I was spinning back in time to the most terrifying night of my life. With a hard mental shake, I forced myself to focus.

"I think I'm okay. I must've hit my head," she murmured as she lifted her hand and brushed at the streak of blood on her cheek.

"Anything else hurt?"

She started to move, and I tightened my grip on her wrist. "Wait. First let me know how you feel."

Her gaze met mine again. If I got through this without having a heart attack, it'd be a damn miracle.

"I think I'm fine. Let me..."

"Ella! Take it slow," I said abruptly when she started to scramble out from where she was pinned.

"Still bossy, I see," she said with a wobbly smile.

I had just about gotten a grip on myself. Hell, I was a hotshot firefighter. Assisting someone in a car accident was easy work for me. Or should've been. But this was Ella, and we had history—messy history that included another car accident, one not so minor and one that tore us apart. The moment a tear rolled down her cheek, I was done for.

"Ella, don't cry," I managed over the tightness in my throat. "You're gonna be fine. Move slowly, and I'll get you out of here."

As if fate was shining a ray on us, the rain lightened up slightly. The next few minutes were a jumble. I managed to help Ella out of the car, right about the time the emergency crew arrived.

Beck Steele, who I'd known since we were in elementary school, all but shoved me out of the way when he realized who I'd helped out of the car. Beck headed up one of the crews at Willow Brook Fire & Rescue, while I was a foreman on another crew. Ella's older brother Cade headed up yet another crew. It was a bittersweet reality to work with Ella's older brother.

All of that spun through my mind while Beck started directing his crew to deal with Ella's likely totaled car. "You're damn lucky she was okay to pull out," he muttered in my ear after she was escorted over to the ambulance to get checked out by the EMT's.

"Fuck off," I mumbled. "You'd have done the same damn thing. I checked on her first. As you can see, she was safe to get out of the vehicle."

Beck rested a hand on his hip, swatting at the rain falling from the sky as if he could make it stop. "I probably would've," he said after a beat. "You know if Maisie called Cade?"

"She said she would. I'll..."

Beck shook his head sharply. "Don't call him. Let Maisie take care of it. She'll be online with the EMT's to give him the latest update. For now, get the hell out of here. You're not on duty."

Watching him walk away, I spun around and strode to the ambulance. Ella was seated on the back edge. Reaching her side, I paused in front of her. "You okay?"

My heart kicked up a notch just being close to her. It had been five years since I'd seen Ella. She looked up at me through the rain, her green eyes bright in the gray light.

"I think so. Dana said I just need a few stitches, right?" she asked, her gaze swinging to Dana Halloran, one of the EMT's on the scene.

Dana nodded from where she stood, turning back to Ella, her eyes bouncing between us briefly. She squirted disinfectant on a cotton ball, carefully dabbing at the cut on the side of Ella's forehead. "That looks like all you'll need. I'll just clean this up and we'll get going. They'll take care of the stitches at the hospital."

Ella looked back at me. "See, just a few stitches," she said.

"I'll meet you at the hospital," I replied as Dana carefully taped a piece of gauze over the cut.

"You don't need to do that," Ella replied.

Dana stepped away and spoke to the ambulance driver. I focused on Ella. "I'll meet you there," I repeated.

"Caleb, you don't have to take care of me. I'm..."

A flash of anger rose inside. I might not have been thinking too clearly, but for God's sake. Ella had once meant everything to me. Then, everything went to hell.

"Ella, you just had a car accident. Is it absolutely necessary to act like we mean nothing to each other?"

ELLA

Waiting in the cold room, I hugged my arms around my waist, trying to will the chill away. I was tired, so very tired. I was also cold and damp. My emotions were pressing against my skin. I wanted to hold them in, but I was all out of strength. I felt ragged and raw. Of all the things to happen today, I had a stupid car accident. I was so close to home, so anxious to get there, I hadn't been paying attention to how fast I was going. Again. I took that corner on the highway and skidded out of control on the slick surface of the road, my car tumbling into the ditch.

And who showed up to rescue me? Caleb Fox. The one and only man I'd never forgotten. What were the chances? To say our history was messy didn't quite capture it. Today was the second time in my life Caleb had pulled me out of a wrecked car. The last time, the car had been on fire, and I'd almost died. Yet, I'd been lucky. Caleb's best friend had died in that same accident.

I didn't realize I was crying until I felt the hot tears rolling down my cheeks. Spinning around, I grabbed a tissue from the box on the counter running along the wall. This room felt so oddly familiar, probably because I'd spent three weeks in the hospital after that last accident. Hospitals had a weird, cold, sterile feeling to them. It was strangely comforting to me.

My stitches were done, and I was ready to go, but they told me to wait until the nurse returned to clear me for discharge. The tissue balled in my hand, I let myself cry for a few minutes. I was all alone, literally and figuratively.

Leaning my hips against the table, I sobbed. I was running home, and I'd been so desperate to get here, I'd completely forgotten to consider that Caleb might be around. Sobs wracked my shoulders, and my head ached from whatever I'd banged into when my car rolled into the ditch.

Get it together, Ella. It's no biggie. You and Caleb have a past, but that's all it is. You can face him. After what you've been through lately, you can handle this.

On the heels of a shuddering breath, I wiped my tears away and tossed the tissue in the wastebasket by the door.

There was a soft knock. Assuming it was the nurse coming to tell me I could finally leave, I called out, "Come in."

Instead of the nurse, Caleb stepped through the door. The moment I laid eyes on him, my pulse lunged. Somehow, I'd forgotten how ridiculously handsome he was. He had straight brown hair that he kept cropped close to his head with chocolate brown eyes. My eyes coasted over him, absorbing the sight of his familiar face with its clean lines—a strong, square jaw, full lips, cheekbones that looked sculpted from stone, and a blade of a nose. As if his face wasn't enough, he had a body of pure muscle. In his faded jeans and damp T-shirt, not much was hidden. The fabric caressed him the way my hands itched to do so.

"Hey, just stopped by to check on you," he said, his voice like honeyed whiskey.

Tears pricked at the backs of my eyes, but I swallowed, forcing the emotion away. I would *not* fall apart in front of him.

"Hey," I croaked.

The room wasn't very big, so when he took a few steps, he was right in front of me. Oh geez. I could smell him—that crisp scent of spruce he seemed to carry with him. I took a deep breath, by force of will keeping my eyes on him.

"How do you feel?" he asked, stuffing his hands in his pockets.

Tightening my arms around my waist, I shrugged. "Fine. They stitched me up and said I'd be cleared to go soon. I'm just waiting, but it's taking forever."

He nodded, his eyes scanning me. This was so weird. The

last time I'd been in the hospital and Caleb came to see me, we'd broken up.

We stood in silence for a beat. Again, I was only alerted to my tears when I felt them on my cheeks. Then, Caleb was right there, wrapping me in his arms. This time, I cried like I hadn't cried in years. Burying my face in his chest, I threw my arms around his waist and hung on. This was about so much more than my stupid roll into a ditch. It was years of missing him and wishing I could fix everything I'd messed up before. It was all of that and the fact I finally felt safe for the first time in years.

He simply held me, one hand tangled in my damp hair and the other circling on my back. He murmured soothing sounds and didn't stop to ask what was wrong or anything. Thank God because I didn't think I could handle that. Not just yet.

After I didn't know how long, I slowly pulled my face away from his chest and looked up. "I got your shirt wet," I mumbled.

Caleb glanced down at me, the corner of his mouth curling up and sending my belly into a few somersaults. "Pretty sure it was already wet."

We stared at each other. After a beat, his gaze sobered. "You okay?"

I shook my head, but I couldn't seem to speak.

His eyes widened in alarm. "Let me get the nurse."

He started to pull away, but I tightened my arms on his waist, shaking my head again. "It's not that. It's just been a shitty day..."

I forced myself to stop talking. I didn't need Caleb, of all people, to know how much I'd stumbled in life. I'd already sent his life careening sideways once before.

"What is it?" he asked, his eyes searing into me. "If you need anything, you know all you have to do is ask."

I almost burst into tears again. Because that was *so* Caleb —he was just a solid guy with a heart of gold and I'd fucked it all up. Everything about him and who he was felt so much bigger in this moment. I'd come running home after five years because I'd stumbled into a nightmare.

"Nothing. There's nothing you can do. I'm just so glad you're here," I said. I meant it, so sincerely it made my heart hurt.

He loosened his hand in my hair and brushed a few locks away from my forehead, checking the bandage there. The cut was right along my hairline, so I was hoping the scar wouldn't be too bad.

"Tell me what's wrong," he said, his tone so careful I almost cried all over again.

I wanted to tell him, but I couldn't. It was too embarrassing.

We stared at each other again. Oh God. It felt so good to be close to him. For the first time in years, I felt like I could relax. I wanted to wrap myself in Caleb and stay there forever.

My next words startled me. "I miss you." The moment those words escaped, I wanted to grab them and stuff them back inside. I didn't need to blurt out all kinds of crazy, emotional stuff.

Caleb stared at me, the hand circling on my back finally pausing. He swallowed, the sound audible in the room. My awareness of him was so heightened the hair on the back of my neck stood up. "You have no idea how much I've missed you," he nearly growled.

Emotion was rushing through me, mingling with desire that should've seemed out of place given everything that had happened, but it didn't. This was me, this was Caleb. Us. There had never been anyone but him in my heart, and my body knew it. He strummed every chord of my being simply by existing in space and time near me.

With a muttered imprecation, he dipped his head, kissing one corner of my mouth and then the other. Oh geez. I was a sucker for corner kisses, at least when it came to him. But then, he'd been the last man I'd kissed, so I didn't really have any comparison. Two more kisses dusted at the corners of my mouth and then I sighed. His tongue swiped along the seam of my lips, and I let go with a low moan.

I held onto him as if he was a life raft in the middle of the ocean, burrowing into him as our tongues tangled. My heart was beating so fast, I could barely breathe. A pager call came over the hospital speakers, and he drew back slowly, his forehead falling to mine.

We stood like that, our breath coming in heaves. Placing my palm on his chest, I felt his heartbeat racing madly just like mine.

Available now!
Burn So Good

Go here to sign up for information on new releases: http://jhcroixauthor.com/subscribe/

FIND MY BOOKS

Thank you for reading Hot Mess! I hope you enjoyed the story. If so, you can help other readers find my books in a variety of ways.

1) Write a review!
2) Sign up for my newsletter, so you can receive information about upcoming new releases & receive a FREE copy of one of my books: http://jhcroixauthor.com/subscribe/
3) Like and follow my Amazon Author page at https://amazon.com/author/jhcroix
4) Follow me on Bookbub at https://www.bookbub.com/authors/j-h-croix
5) Follow me on Twitter at https://twitter.com/JHCroix
6) Like my Facebook page at https://www.facebook.com/jhcroix

Into The Fire Series
Burn For Me
Slow Burn
Burn So Bad
Hot Mess
Burn So Good
Sweet Fire
Play With Fire
Melt With You

Brit Boys Sports Romance
The Play
Big Win
Out Of Bounds
Play Me
Naughty Wish

Diamond Creek Alaska Novels
When Love Comes
Follow Love
Love Unbroken
Love Untamed
Tumble Into Love
Christmas Nights

Last Frontier Lodge Novels
Take Me Home
Love at Last
Just This Once
Falling Fast
Stay With Me
When We Fall
Hold Me Close
Crazy For You

Catamount Lion Shifters
Protected Mate
Chosen Mate
Fated Mate

Destined Mate
A Catamount Christmas
Ghost Cat Shifters
The Lion Within
Lion Lost & Found

ACKNOWLEDGMENTS

To my girls who help me get every day off to a running start, who shower me with wags and kisses and who are the best dog friends ever.

Many thanks to Yoly Cortez who is so gracious as she makes magic with my covers. My proofreader angels keep an eye out for me, literally - Janine, Beth P., Terri D., Terri E., Heather H., & Carolyne B. - many thanks!

A bow of thanks to my readers who make it possible for me to do this! I'm almost convinced some of you telepathically communicate and know just when I need an email telling me you loved one of my stories.

Of course, DBC - my touchstone. You are always there through the good, the bad, and the messy. Thank you doesn't seem sufficient.

xoxo

J.H. Croix

ABOUT THE AUTHOR

USA Today Bestselling Author J. H. Croix lives in a small town in the historical farmlands of Maine with her husband and two spoiled dogs. Croix writes steamy contemporary romance with sassy women and alpha men who aren't afraid to show some emotion. Her love for quirky small-towns and the characters that inhabit them shines through in her writing. Take a walk on the wild side of romance with her bestselling novels!

Places you can find me:
jhcroixauthor.com
jhcroix@jhcroix.com

facebook.com/jhcroix
twitter.com/jhcroix

Printed in Great Britain
by Amazon